10/16

MAGGIE ON THE BOUNTY

BOOK III
MAGGIE MACKAY
MAGICAL TRACKER SERIES

by Kate Danley

This is a work of fiction. All of the characters, organizations, and events portrayed in this novel are either products of the author's imagination or are used fictitiously.

First Printing

Cover Art Image by LFD Author Design

WITH SPECIAL THANKS TO

MY ANGELS OF THE NIGHT OF WRITING DANGEROUSLY

Christy & Tyler Wilhelm

C.L. Jones

Corny Koehl

The Danley Family

CHAPTER ONE

A week ago, the lives of my mom, dad, and sister were on the line. I battled a horde of vampires-turned-werewolf and werewolves-turned-vampire, in the middle of a ghost town filled with people-turned-ghost. I faced down the biggest, baddest vampire of them all, a jerk named Vaclav. I also had to kill my employer, a guy named Mr. Smith. It's okay. He was evil.

It sounds like a pretty action-packed weekend, but it's kinda turning into how I spend my Saturdays.

My name is Maggie MacKay. I'm a magical tracker.

I live in an alternate dimension called The Other Side, but have earned enough Frequent Portal Points for all the jumps I make between The Other Side and Earth to almost qualify for a Dyson.

Whenever monsters decide to invade Los Angeles, I get the call to haul them back. It's like being the permanent designated driver for a bunch of asshole frat boys... with fangs...

Mind you, things have been a little hairier than normal these past few months, and I ain't just talkin' werewolves. It started with vampires. The werewolves came after. And then the vampires bit the werewolves and the werewolves bit the vampires and now I've got a horde of creatures that can only be killed by silver stakes, all gunning at me.

And that was nothing compared to the terror in my heart at this moment.

"It is only brunch," Killian said to me from the passenger seat of my car.

Since my sister's "family dinner" had been destroyed last week, you know, because we were mildly busy saving the world, Mindy called for a do-over. She was pretending it was a celebration of my dad's retirement. I got the feeling it was more to make sure no stakings happened on a Sunday. From the tone of her voice, she acted as if we owed her. You let your sister get possessed one lousy time...

"Think of all the towers of pastries," Killian encouraged. "You enjoy a good pastry."

The latest employee at MacKay & MacKay Tracking was a 6'5 blonde elf named Killian. Some get distracted by his rakish good looks, but once you quit being blinded by his beauty, you usually just want to punch him. We've been through some pretty big adventures together, though, so I let him stick around. Okay, truth be told, I more than just let him stick around, I invited him to be my new partner. We still haven't picked out stationery logos, but that's what a family brunch is for, right? Awkward questions about your future and thinly veiled inquiries about when they are going to hear the pitter-patter of tiny franchise opportunities. It's enough to make a girl open up a portal and let herself be swallowed up by another world.

Which I could do. I'm able to open up portals between dimensions like nobody's business. Okay, so my dad is better than me. What can I say? He's had a bit more practice. But now that he's retired, the only thing he is going to be opening are tea bags at my mom's psychic eye tea shop, Leaf It Be, on The Other Side. My completely normal twin sister, Mindy, lives a completely normal life as an accountant in Pasadena with a completely normal and totally nice husband, Austin, and a completely normal dog. Oh, my sister does have a brownie named Pipistrelle, who is so adorable you might be able to count him as a pet. He was looking for a good excuse to stick around Earth; she was looking for someone to clean the baseboards. Pipistrelle LOVES cleaning baseboards.

"You know Pipistrelle can cook these chefs under the table. I don't see why Mindy decided to have a family gathering sixty miles from where any family actually lives."

"Really, Maggie, this shall be a most delightful human experience. Why so ill-tempered?"

I looked at him in disbelief. "It is 9:00 a.m. on a Sunday morning and we have just spent the past hour battling it through all the weekend warriors returning from The Other Side to Earth, not to mention traffic on the 710 Freeway down to Long Beach, all so that we can eat an omelet. I'm tired. I'm cranky. And I'm wearing a skirt."

Killian looked at me and remarked, "It is a lovely skirt. Black continues to be your color."

"I can't think in a skirt, Killian."

"I have difficulty thinking when you are in a skirt, too."

"Shut up, elf."

So down in Long Beach is this great big cruise ship built in the 1930's by the same folks who put together the Titanic. Fortunately, this boat didn't make any claims about unsinkableness and Murphy's Law didn't feel the need to come out and prove a point.

So, this boat chugged along happily for a number of years. It was an ocean liner for the rich and famous in the 1930's. Shuttled soldiers across the ocean to fight the bad guys in the 1940's. And then in the 70's, it was sailed through the Panama Canal and docked in Long Beach, where it was turned into a floating hotel and the best Sunday brunch you'll find west of the Atlantic Ocean.

"Your mother and father are meeting us on the ship?" Killian asked.

"Yeah, Mom and Dad stayed with Mindy last night. Lucky sons of guns."

Killian looked at me. "That makes no sense. Your mother is a woman."

Elves.

So, Killian was actually better than most of his type I've dealt with. Usually these elves are off gallivanting through the forest, braiding flowers in each other's hair. If push came to shove, I don't think he'd be above making a daisy chain, but I know he'd never try to stick it on my head, and I think that's what true friendship is about.

Elves have their own elfish language, but Killian was a multicultural Other Side Language studies major in school, so he can usually hold his own. Usually. I do my best to fill in any educational gaps whenever I got the chance.

"Fuck it.   Hopefully someone will meet me at the door with a cup full of coffee and we can pretend that this morning was nothing more than some terrible dream."

We pulled into the parking lot. In front of us was a massive, white, sun-damaged geodesic dome that once housed the Spruce Goose, the largest plane that ever flew, albeit for just a couple seconds. Now it is used for storage or conference space or something. Beyond it is a cute little half-timbered village that looked a bit like a Renaissance Festival of abandoned shops. I think there might be a copy place still open, but I'd be surprised. Beyond the little village is a port, usually filled with modern cruise ships ready to set sail for three glorious days to the Mexican Rivera. Today it was empty.

The only boat left was the Empress Adelaide, her three red smokestacks against the blue sky, sitting proudly in front of the city of Long Beach in a manmade harbor with a fake little fishing village and a fake little lighthouse atop a fake hill overlooking a mural of fake humpback whales all overlooking a fake little island where they processed garbage. I'm sure it would have been more charming if I had some caffeine in my system.

We parked in the open-air lot. The sun was shining all cheerfully, like I should be happy to be alive or some such crap. I went to the trunk of my car and pulled out my gun.

"Now, Maggie. This is brunch."

I felt like Killian didn't even know me. "Right. This is brunch."

I stashed an extra round in my purse.

"Leave the bullets," he commanded.

"You ruin everything, Killian," I said as I pulled them out and put them back.

He shook his head. "And the throwing stars."

I removed a couple from inside my wristband. "Happy?" I asked.

"All of them."

I sighed and pulled the hidden one out of the lining of my bag.

"Thank you," he said. He came and put his arm around my shoulders bracingly, "Just think—a family meal without being armed to the teeth. I believe you might be setting a precedent."

"My dad gets to be armed," I pointed out.

"Sometimes you must allow the elders to be in charge," Killian soothed. He looked up at the ship. "Now, tell me about this place?"

"It is a hotel. It has brunch. It's haunted—"

"Haunted?" asked Killian. He stopped in the middle of the parking lot. "And your sister decided this was the ideal spot to gather your family together for a quiet Sunday meal?"

I could see a flicker of apprehension cross his face, the big baby.

"Bet you're wishing you had let me come armed," I said.

"Not when your mother is around," he replied.

Now that we were off the road and the diesel-desert-dust in my lungs got shoved aside for a little oxygen and sea air, I started feeling better about this. The fact that Killian was starting to squirm was pure icing on the cake. Frosting, even. Buttercream frosting on fluffy red velvet cake. Haunted, shmaunted—I was hungry.

"They do make a mean omelet," I admitted.

"I do not understand," said Killian.

"You will."

We walked over to the gold carpet they have set up for visitors. The carpet leads to an industrial tower structure of white pipes and corrugated metal built on the outside of the boat. It houses the elevator that takes you to the various ship levels, then you walk across a bridge to check out the inside. Mindy and I had been making wishes and chucking pennies off the outside walkways since we were little. Right now, I only wished for caffeine.

"What does your mother feel about this place?"

I shrugged. "She's actually never seen anyone ghostly on the premises. Swears this is all just a big tourist trap. Who knows."

The door to the elevator opened, and standing in front of me was the familiar face of an old Irish priest.

"Father Killarney!" I exclaimed.

His face lit up as he broke out in his Irish brogue, "Maggie-girl!"

Maybe this brunch wasn't going to suck as much as I thought it would.

Father Killarney is an old Irish-Catholic priest and long-time friend of the family. Turns out he knew my dad and my uncle way back before they even picked out whether to use their powers for good or evil. Father Killarney also runs a cleanup crew and is on call whenever I need something sent back to hell.

I hurried inside the elevator and gave him a great big hug. He reached out and grabbed Killian, bringing him into our group bear hug, too.

"Hand off my ass, elf," I muttered under my

breath at Killian.

Father Killarney broke away, gazing at us like we were more miraculous than a Bob Ross painting. He ruffled Killian's hair. "I see you decided to keep the elf around, did you Maggie?" said Father Killarney, a bit too delighted.

"We just got him house trained," I replied.

Killian pinched me.

"Ah! You are such a sight for sore eyes!" Father Killarney exclaimed, coming back to earth. "So, how are the two of you doing? You been off battling the forces of darkness again?"

I shrugged as I pressed the elevator button for the third floor. "Oh, the usual. Foiled Vaclav. Had a little altercation out in Ghost Town. There was a thing with some werepires and vampwolves. And that's about it. You?"

"Oh, always one thing if it is not the other here in this town," he said, shaking his head.

"I didn't know you would be here," I said. "Isn't Sunday supposed to be kind of a busy day in the work-schedule for you priests and stuff?"

"I pulled the early shift. There is a wedding this afternoon, right here on the Empress Adelaide. Worked it out perfectly so that I could also minister to your family."

The elevator ground to a halt and we stepped out onto the concrete bridge—not a ship bridge, just a bridge-bridge—and walked over to the boat.

"Are you sure you're not ministering to the free breakfast?"

"That is between me and my Lord. But if your soul needs settling as to the purity of my motivations, I am more than happy to minister to you now. I noticed you were not in one of my pews this morning..."

I cut him off. "I will be worshipping at the holy altar of the dessert station, Father. I hear someone saw the face of God in a crepe. I'm here to investigate that his permits are in order."

"And I shall be happy to re-hallow the flan if it proves necessary," Father Killarney laughed. He then took my elbow and steered me along. He whispered gently as we walked through the door and into the boat proper, "Maggie-girl, you forgot to take your neck guard off."

I reached up, felt the Kevlar, and groaned. Nobody would really care, but it had about as much couth as wearing a flak jacket to Thanksgiving.

"Killian! I'm going to the little girls' room!" I announced as I ditched the boys in the lobby near the grand ballroom. I walked past two art deco elevators made of chrome and birds-eye paneling. Parked next to the far elevator was a bored-looking photographer, snagging guests as they came through to commemorate this trip to nowhere. I kept walking towards the portholes and turned left before I fell into the ocean.

Hanging on the wall was a painting of a lovely old broad dressed in a white flowing gown and sash draped across the front. The dress was gauzy and flowed about her like the painter had turned on a fan to capture the sexy. *Allure*, eat your heart out. Her grey hair was short and kept in tight curls close to her head. Perched atop was a delicate little tiara.

"Empress Adelaide I presume?" I smiled as I passed.

It smiled back.

KATE DANLEY

Now, I know about the whole Mona Lisa thing, where she semi-smiles at you and her eyes follow you around the room or whatever, but there's a difference between oil-paint tricks and actual twitches at the corner of a mouth. I stopped and walked right up to that portrait and stared it in the eyes.

No bells and whistles went off in my head. My tracker senses didn't scream, "MAGIC!" at me. It seemed like just a normal old painting. Mom swore this place was about as psychically active as a petting zoo, but there were plenty of other types of ghoulies that might have taken up residence.

"I'm here with my family for brunch when I could be at home in bed," I warned. "I haven't had any coffee yet and I'm armed. If you mess with me today, I swear to God I'll make sure you're hung in a basement."

The painting definitely didn't move.

I gave her one last don't-make-me-put-you-in-time-out-young-lady glance before going on to the restroom.

Restoration dollars only go so far, and this powder room sported a look that could only be described as high school teacher's lounge chic. Lots of cheap, gold-flecked Formica and industrial naugahyde chairs. I stood looking in the chipped mirror, my fingers on the locks of my neck guard, thinking about that stupid painting and trying to ignore my gut-instinct not to take the thing off. I really didn't know if this was such a good idea anymore. If I was going without a neck guard, I should at least have something sharper than a grapefruit spoon. But my brain went through the laundry list: The painting really hadn't moved. I was brunching with a priest on a Sunday, so that should count for something. And if I showed up at the table looking like things were going to go down at 10 a.m., it would put a damper on my sister's plans. That's what settled it. I wasn't going to give her ammunition for another do-over.

I spun the locks on the neck guard and let it fall into my hands. I took a minute to massage the red marks on my neck where it had pressed too long against my skin.

If I got killed at brunch at least I would die with waffles in my belly, I told myself as I walked back out toward the lobby. There are worse ways to go, and only one or two better. After all, you only live once.

"Maggie! Black to brunch? You look like something straight out of the Dark Dimension," scolded a familiar voice.

Although sometimes once is enough.

"Hey, Mom!"

She came over and squeezed me tight. She was wearing her good pink muumuu with the yellow hibiscus flowers.

"Good to see you, too," I said, kissing her on the cheek.

"A little color wouldn't make you look so pale and washed out."

I sighed. "As we've talked about, it's hard to hide in shadows from the vampires when you are wearing fuchsia." I put the neck guard in my purse next to where my stake and handgun should have been. Stupid Killian.

"Bah. Vampires. It's the middle of the morning, Maggie," Mom proclaimed.

"A MacKay is always prepared," I reminded her.

She shook her head as if she couldn't believe she

had raised a daughter who would place survival over fashion.

She fluffed her orange curls, recently having traded in her triangle haircut for something more helmet like. Her transformation into Mrs. Roper was almost complete. Everyone has to have heroes, I guess.

"Hey, Mom?" I asked.

"Hmmm?" she replied as she pulled out her coral lipstick.

"Have you been feeling anything funny since you got on the ship?"

She shook her head. "No. Not a thing. Why? Did you feel something funny?" She turned to me, her eyes suddenly lit up. "Oh do tell! I keep hoping that someday your gift will wake up. Did it wake up? You can tell me!"

"Right." I cleared my throat, "So, I was walking past a painting in the hallway and it looked like it smiled at me."

"What?" Mom asked, suddenly looking concerned. "Why don't you show it to me?"

We walked out into the hallway and I stopped. The painting wasn't there. I mean, the whole thing was gone. Not a frame. Not a hook. Not a nail. Nothing. In fact, the lovely wall it had been hanging on was missing, too, and in its place was an accordion divider.

"It was right here," I swore. I pulled back the divider and there was no wall behind it, just the ballroom set up for brunch and all of its normal, mortal eaters.

Mom felt my forehead. "You don't seem to be running a fever."

I brushed off her hand. "I'm fine. There was a

painting here. And it is gone and so is the wall."

She looked around. "Are you sure this is where you saw it?"

"I am pretty sure." I stared at the spot I was sure it was at. "Maybe I got turned around."

"Do you feel anything strange about this place? Any fluctuations? Any indications someone is tampering with the border?"

I shook my head again. "No. Nothing. It feels so completely normal, I'd think that this place had never even heard of The Other Side. You?"

She patted my shoulder. "It will be okay. You've been under so much stress lately..."

"Mo-o-om..."

"Hunting vampires is hard! You freed all the citizens of that Ghost Town, and you haven't stopped since! You haven't had a break in a week..."

"It's not that big of a deal."

She kissed my temple. "It is to me. Now, let's go see what sort of omelets they serve before those boys go and eat everything."

She linked her arm in mine and walked me to the ballroom.

Dad was in the lobby waiting for us, talking up a storm with my twin, Mindy, and her hubby, Austin. Killian and Father Killarney had already found their way over to the merry crew. It was like the setup for a "priest, an elf, and a world walker went into a bar" joke.

"You mob got your buffet pants on?" I asked, showing them the elastic waistband on my skirt.

I was greeted with cheers and we headed on in. A row of waiters in white dinner jackets stood at the ready, lined up smartly next to the check-in desk to walk us to our seats.

"Very fancy," I whispered to Mindy.

"Try not to spill all over yourself," she muttered back.

Our host walked us to our table. It was dressed up in a linen tablecloth and had a good view of the ice sculptures. The Grand Ballroom, itself, was an art deco wonderland. The walls were inlaid wood and the two-story ceiling was held up with veneer columns. Murals were everywhere you looked. Lots of faux Asian flair: herons and whooping cranes and orchids. On one side of the room was a great big painting of New York to Paris, with a brass track connecting the two and a little boat riding the track. I pointed it out to Killian. "So when this boat used to travel back and forth, they would position the boat up there so the passengers could see how far along they were on their trip."

Killian nodded appreciatively. "Quite ingenious for such a primitive culture."

"We can't all be elves."

"Pity."

"We did, however, invent the Belgian waffle, which I've never heard served of in your forest."

"Bah! Waffles! Pipistrelle introduced me to an item called 'cheesecake.' Do you think they have such a construct here?"

I patted Killian on the shoulder. "I like the way you think, elf."

Mindy shook her head. "Dessert?"

"With the way my life tends to go, I'm just hedging my bets. It sure would suck if the last meal in my life was salad."

"Touché. Dessert it is!"

The center of the room featured a parquet floor and more food stations than any single nation had an excuse to own—omelets to order, seafood, make your own crepes, Chinese food, prime rib, Build-a-Breakfast Burritos—you name it, they had it. The waitstaff kept our glasses filled with coffee and fresh squeezed orange juice. They offered champagne and stopped by frequently enough, I didn't even have to ask them to leave the bottle. All in all, even grumpy-pants me had to admit it was a pretty fantastic brunch.

"So you have visited this vessel before?" Killian asked.

My mom nodded. "Oh, I used to come here quite often, but I don't think William ever has."

Dad took a bite of his seafood salad and shook his head, "Nope, this is my first trip."

"We discovered this place back when he was caught in the boundary," Mom explained.

"If I had known, I would have worked harder to get out," Dad said, swallowing and then diving into his pile of peel-and-eat shrimp.

Father Killarney pushed himself back from the table and folded his hands upon his belly. He looked up at the ceiling and got a dreamy look in his eye. I braced myself. The man was about to wax on about something. I motioned to the waiter to bring me more booze.

"Oh, the Empress Adelaide used to shuttle movie stars across the Atlantic, pretty as you please, but during the war, they painted her the color of the fog and filled her with soldiers. Packed them in like sardines. And wouldn't you know, though she was chased by every U-Boat in the sea, this beautiful lady stayed just out of their grasp. There was quite a bounty on her head back in the day. They used to call her the Ghost Spirit."

I looked around the grand dining room. "Ghost Spirit, huh?"

"Said that it was like she vanished out there and nothin' but the sea would be left behind."

Mindy wiped a bit of chocolate from her lip. "I hear they have a ghost tour... We should go!" She waved her fingers like it was all spooky.

Mom threw down her napkin in disgust. "Well."

I gave her a sideways look. "Really?"

"I don't like people who use the dead as a money-making device."

I thought back to her psychic eye shop over on The Other Side. "You use the dead as a money-making device."

"My shop is not some haunted house."

"It actually is, literally, a haunted house..." I pointed out.

"That is beside the point. I speak with the real, actual dead and connect them with their family members or help them to cross to the world beyond. This is pure exploitation and makes a mockery of my profession and gifts."

"Come now, dear," my dad tried to soothe, "it is just a bit of fun."

"Just you wait until they start building a bunch of fun houses where people can create fake portals in the wall. Hand them a sledgehammer and some dry wall and tell them they are jumping dimensions!"

"That actually sounds like a really good time," Mindy said. It actually did. You can never go wrong with a little recreational demolition.

Mom looked like she was about to get on a rant about the proper and improper use of ghosts as party tricks when Austin, God bless him, took his glass and tapped it with his knife. We all looked over at him.

"There is a reason we hauled you all out here," he said.

Mindy reached over and grabbed Austin's hand. "There is..."

"You're pregnant!" laughed Mom.

I dropped my fork loudly on the table. "What?"

"MOM! I wanted to tell everyone!"

"Oh, Mindy! It is so wonderful!" Mom said, running over to kiss her all over her cheeks. Dad reached over to shake Austin's hand.

"I am so sorry for dropping you through the roof of Ghost Town," I apologized.

Mindy waved it off. "Killian broke my fall."

Austin pointed his butter knife at me. "But no more getting my wife into these sorts of situations again. She's staking for two right now."

"Maggie it will be your turn next," Mom said with a wink.

Killian gave me a meaningful look and I kicked him under the table.

"It would be so nice if Mindy's baby had someone to play with," she continued.

"The only thing I want in my belly," I informed her, "is more dessert." I pointed at Mindy's plate. "Pass me your brownie."

"Pipistrelle stays with me," my sister warned.

"Ha ha. Your dessert plate. Fork it over. There are starving children in the world and I need to rub it in their faces I have caramel and they don't."

Killian shook his head. "Always a picture of tact

and decorum."

"It is a wonder I don't work for the UN. Now, pass it over."

As Mom and Dad talked to Mindy and Austin about all of the ins and outs of organizing a cross-dimensional daycare and which car seat is best when running your car off of Mulholland, I leaned over to Father Killarney and whispered, "You haven't come across anything in your studies about... baby issues... when a mom is possessed by evil genie Dark Side magic, right?"

Killian took a meaningful swig from his mimosa.

"What are you talking about, Maggie-girl?" the priest asked.

"Just a little something that happened while we were in Ghost Town."

Father Killarney shook his head. "I'll see what I can find out and let you know."

"Guess we'll just see what we're in for a bit down the road," I replied.

"Maybe there's a little something I can do in the interim." Father Killarney wiped his mouth with his napkin. "Mindy! An Irish blessing on that beautiful belly of yours! Get over here!"

Mindy walked over and Father Killarney hovered his hands over her abdomen. "A blessing on this wee babe. In the Lord's name I cast out all demons and dark shadows and give this child over to the light." He made the sign of the cross over his water goblet and then dipped his fingers in and flung the water droplets on Mindy.

Mindy gave him a look. "That was a funny blessing, Father Killarney."

He stood and gave her a kiss on the forehead.

"You have a funny family."

Mindy's hand went to her womb, suddenly distracted. "Oh! It moved!"

Mom and Dad were instantly cooing and the blessing took a backseat to this new development. I tried to tell myself the timing had nothing to do with Father Killarney's words.

Since he was already standing, Father Killarney dried his hands and announced. "Well, 'tis a shame, but this couple isn't going to marry itself and I'm afraid my duties call." He gave handshakes and cheek smooches all around. "It was a pleasure! Until next time. And Mindy, know that the moment that baby comes out, I'll be waiting with a bowl of water to get it good and baptized for you. No group baptisms for the MacKay girls!"

When he came to me, he leaned over and whispered in my ear, "You keep an eye on her. You tell me if you see anything strange."

"Sure thing, Father Killarney!" I chirped back, probably a bit too chirpy.

Mindy watched him as he left and shook her head, sort of bemused. "That was weird."

"Let's go look around the ship!" I suggested, trying to change the subject, probably a bit too subject-changily.

That was two "bit too"s in a row and the family was starting to look at me strangely. One more and someone was going to call me on my bullshit. I just got up, hoping folks would follow suit.

Austin gave Mindy a kiss. "Like the priest said. You're a weird family."

We left the ballroom and took the elevator up to the promenade deck. It was this indoor/outdoor stretch of dark-planked wood that went the entire length of the boat. The place was so huge, you could totally play a game of football. A very, very narrow game of football. It was covered, but the walls were open to the outside so that passengers could go get some fresh air without the sun beating down upon their heads. There were deck chairs and little shops, a couple of displays showing off pictures of what the boat used to look like and the celebrities who once sailed upon her.

Her story morphed into her days as the Ghost Spirit army ship. There were pictures of thousands of army troops smooshed shoulder-to-shoulder on her decks. I looked at the photograph of all the soldiers stacked into their bunks like sardines and my breath stopped. I recognized one of the guys.

"Hey, look! It is Rex Turner!" I said, laughing.

"Who is that?" Mindy asked.

Dad elbowed his way forward and squinted through the Plexiglas. "So it is!"

"Vampire we hauled in last Christmas. He got a job playing Santa at the mall. Whenever the grownups would come sit on his lap, he'd get himself a little Christmas cheer, too. The CDC thought it was an outbreak of the bird flu. Folks were blaming the bites on monster mosquitoes or something."

"Ho ho ho," said Mindy sardonically as she looked closer at the picture.

"And to think we're walking the very same planks he walked. Wonder what other vampires used this boat to cross the Atlantic?"

"No telling," said my dad, wrapping his arm around Mom's shoulder. "Who knows... there could be one here right now." He bit her neck playfully and she squealed like a thirteen- year-old girl.

I covered Killian's eyes. "You're not ready for this horror, elf."

We headed topside and got a chance to look into the bridge and Captain's quarters. They still had some of the old guns that the military mounted on the front deck. They were big enough to take down an airplane, but covered in so many layers of lead-based paint, it was pretty clear their days of service were long since over. Up near the smokestacks was a shuffleboard deck and a great view of the city. More towards the back was an old infirmary with a list of all the folks that died on the ship. It totally gave me the creeps, but Mom acted as if it was nothing but an empty old room, so I chalked it up to champagne and general paranoia. Folks started pooping out about the time we hit the poop deck, so we decided to call it quits.

"Aren't you heading out with us?" asked Mom as she gave me a hug.

"I'm going to hit the little girls' room first," I said. The drive to The Other Side was a bit more of a slog than their jaunt up to Pasadena.

Mindy gave me a squeeze. "We'll see you next week!"

"Thanks for breakfast. And congratulations, sis."

"This little one is going to have the safest babysitter on the planet," Austin laughed. "No monsters in the closet this time around!"

Mindy gave me a smile. "You're going to be a great auntie."

"Aw! Get out of here, you crazy kids, before Mindy gestates and has this baby right here on the boat!"

They laughed, pretending I said something far wittier than what actually came out of my mouth, and headed on out. I jerked my head towards the indoor direction and said, "I'll be right back, Killian."

"I shall wait for you here," he replied, leaning against the railing and relaxing, all zen and happy.

Famous last words.

CHAPTER TWO

I walked over to the sink to wash my hands. Despite the ship being a floating museum of days gone by, the loo was a wonderland of modern touchless technology. There was an automatic soap dispenser over the sink, but someone got the timer all mixed up. Every time I moved my hands close, it would sit there staring dumbly at me. When I moved them away, it squirted. I ran my hand beneath it and nada. FINALLY I hit the automatic eye and it shot out a little stream of white foam into my hands. As I ran my hands under the water, suddenly the soap dispenser wouldn't quit spurting at me.

"Technology," I muttered, pulling my hands away to turn off the water.

And then, with the water off, all the soap pooled at the bottom of the sink, then bubbled into a word: "Death."

Fuck.

"A haunted soap dispenser?!?" I shouted. "Are

you fucking kidding me?"

I looked around. I was the only lady in the ladies room so couldn't grab anyone to verify that this was what was going on.

But there it was staring at me: "Death."

I pulled out my phone and snapped a picture. I shook my finger at the bubbles, which weren't going anywhere. "Okay, I don't know who you are or what's going on, but if you're a ghost, you're going to have to talk to my mom. She's the only one who can hear you types."

Nobody appeared.

"If, by some chance, you are referring to the death of my family, however, I will hunt you down and drag you off to a dimension where you will beg to be put out of your misery."

Again nothing.

I walked out of the bathroom and grabbed Killian's shirt.

He looked down at my wet hands. "They have a wondrous invention called a 'towel' nowadays."

"Could I borrow you for just a sec?" I asked, dragging him away before he had a chance to turn me down. I pushed him into the restroom.

"Maggie, I do not believe I should be going in—" Killian stopped and looked in the sink. "Do you care to share with me why the word death was written in soap in the basin of the ladies room?"

"I don't know," I replied. "I was just washing up, the soap dispenser started going crazy, and suddenly I look down and I'm getting death threats. At brunch. What kind of lousy Sunday morning is this?"

"I am sure it is not personal."

"Just an hour ago, I was perfectly happy

consuming a mountain of pancakes. And now some ghost decides to leave me creepy messages?!?"

"At least he did not spell it in syrup on your plate."

"Listen, Mom isn't sensing ghosts. I'm not sensing portals. But, there is something happening because last I checked, SoftSoap's new marketing scheme didn't involve hidden warnings after you pee."

"Did you examine the men's room?"

"No, I didn't go wandering inside the men's room. That seems like more of a task for a man-folk."

"Very well, I shall go and see," Killian said, pulling down the bottom of his shirt and fixing his cuffs. He waved at the exit. "After you."

"You're not scared of ghosts now, are you?" I asked as I pushed him in front of me, maybe hiding just a little behind him and hoping he wouldn't notice.

"Perhaps you would like to join me since you seem to be so 'over' your fear," he suggested, totally calling me out.

"No."

He spun around and booped me on the nose. "I will examine the men's room and ensure the ghost... the coast... is clear."

"Cute."

"A slip of the tongue."

"I'm sure."

"I will ensure the room is empty before you enter."

He pushed on the door and went inside. After a few minutes, I considered just making a run for the car and letting him handle whatever was lurking by himself, but then he peeked his head around the corner. "It is safe, Maggie."

I walked in. It was a lot like the girl's room, except it smelled like boys.

"Now, before someone enters and interrupts us, show me exactly what you did."

I gave him a look. "This is stupid. Next you'll be making me look into the mirror and say 'Bloody Mary' three times."

"What is 'Bloody Mary?'"

"It ain't just a morning cocktail, I'll tell you that much." I looked into the sink. "And if it is Bloody Mary, I swear to God I'll get my mom to lock her up in a purse compact faster than you can say Cover Girl."

I turned on the water. "Okay, so this is what happened. I tried to get the soap out and it wouldn't come out. This soap is coming out just fine, so imagine it didn't, then..."

There was a hissing sound behind us.

We both turned.

The entry door to the bathroom had not opened. Killian had checked all the toilets. We had been completely alone in that room, and yet somehow, there was a fucking vampire coming out of the stalls towards us.

"Bless us, oh Lord and these thy soap!" I shouted at the bubbles in my hand before flinging them at the vampire.

So, yeah, it wasn't as good as holy water, but I just needed a little zap, just long enough to be able to dig through my purse.

"Killian! If you had let me keep those throwing stars, we wouldn't be in this situation!"

The vampire was howling and trying to rub the holy bubbles out of his eyes. Killian grabbed my purse out of my hands as the zipper slipped around in my fingers.

"What do you require?" he asked as his helping completely got in my way.

"Oh, fuck this." I reached between my legs and pulled out the stake I had strapped to my thigh. I winged it at the vampire and caught him dead to rights.

Killian stood there with my purse.

"Thanks for holding my bag," I said, taking it from him.

"I thought I knew everything you were packing today."

"A woman is a mystery, an enigma wrapped in a paradox. Don't ever think you've got us figured out."

I was playing it all cool, but as Killian walked over to inspect the dead dude, my hand touched my unguarded neck. The skin there still bore the marks from a time when I was younger and stupider. It only takes one. And here fashion almost got me killed. I pulled out my neck guard and slapped that puppy around my throat faster than you can say "Jack the Ripper."

Killian was sifting through the guy's pockets. Sometimes they carry around ID. I can't tell you how many times vampires head out on a Friday night to neck with some co-ed at a bar and get foiled by some bouncer because they look eighteen.

Killian confirmed there was nothing in the guy's pants. "He is not dressed in clothing I would expect to see on passengers of this boat."

"Maybe he was one of the lounge acts?" I offered.

Killian was right, though. The vampire was awfully dapper for a Sunday morning, even if it involved mimosas. He had on a three-piece swallow-tailed morning coat, something you'd see straight off of a period piece on the BBC. Or someone from The Other Side who hadn't remembered a change of clothes, indicating we had ourselves what is called an illegal jumper. Which meant he was my problem.

We both stood there, staring.

"We can't leave him here, huh?" I sighed.

Killian shook his head.

"How on earth are we going to get this sucker out without anyone seeing us?"

Killian shook his head again.

"And how did he get in here in the first place?" I asked.

"That answer can wait until later. Right now, we need to remove him before any humans discover that there are monsters among them."

I looked at the vampire, "Ever seen *Weekend at Bernie's*?"

Killian looked at me blankly.

"That was some great 1980's filmmaking. Come on. Hoist this guy's arms over your head. I'm tying his shoelaces to your feet."

Killian looked down, "He does not appear to have shoelaces."

Details. Details.

"Perhaps you could tear your skirt and tie his legs to us that way," Killian said, staring at my mini.

"Or you could give me your socks," I replied.

"I believe in all of the 1980's movies I have seen, the heroine would have listened to her male companion and sacrificed her clothing."

"Shut up, elf."

Killian went into the stall.

"What are you doing?" I called.

"Just as you requested!"

He came out and handed me a wad of material.

I hadn't been thinking.

Despite his decision to go costumed as a human today, elves wear tights.

He handed me his man-hose and stood there shifting himself and looking a little uncomfortable.

"Free as a bird?" I asked as I tied one leg to him and one leg to our dead dude.

"Like a young elf on his first midsummer eve."

"I don't even know what that means."

"Oh, someday you shall," he replied.

"Not if I can help it."

I finished tying the dead guy to me. "Okay, so if anyone asks, he drank too many bloody marys—"

"He drank the ghost in the mirror...?"

"No, the beverage."

"They named a drink after a ghost...?"

"No. Stop it. Just... he drank too much and we're taking him home so he can sleep it off."

"How do you explain the gaping hole in his chest?"

I looked at the spot where my stake had been. "Well, that's unfortunate." I grabbed some paper towels and draped them over his front. "He barfed up his shrimp cocktail. As long as you act normal, Killian, no one will say anything."

I could see Killian was not completely on-board with my brilliant plan.

"Could you not blink him into The Other Side?" Killian asked.

"Tempting, but whatever is through the boundary here is where he calls home, and I'd rather not show up in his living room. Plus, I'm thinking that there might be a nice little reward for us if we bring him back."

Killian nodded, slowly warming to the idea. "I like big rewards."

"AND, I'm thinking we might need to have to make a trip to say hello to Lacy..."

"I like Lacy."

"I thought you might." I swung the dead vampire's arms over Killian and my shoulders, "Come on, partner. We have some bounty money to collect."

"Lead on."

CHAPTER THREE

Lacy looked up from her ledger as I walked in and threw the vampire's body on the reception desk. She rolled her eyes. "You're gonna get vampire juice all over my keyboard, Maggie."

Lacy was a woman who lived the blues. Probably because she was blue. All of her. From the tip of her curly hair to the bottom of her dainty toes. She handled intake over at the prison, but the way she wore her uniform was not regulation. The bedazzled name-tag was a good look. It threw people off from the fact she could wipe the floor with your ass any time she liked.

"Sorry, Lacy. Just wanted to make sure you saw this guy's face before he got lost in the bureaucratic shuffle."

"I like to see his face in the photos from the morgue, not because you've decided he's my new cube-mate."

"I'm not sure this guy is going to be wanted in

your morgue. I need you to do me a solid, Lacy."

She rolled her eyes. "Maggie, when do you NOT want me to do you a solid? It's like I see you coming through the door and I know I'm in for double the paperwork."

The bell rang as Killian walked in.

"What about for me?" he asked.

Lacy purred, "I'd rather you did me a solid."

"That could be arranged," he winked.

"I'm going to throw up," I pointed out.

"Shut up, Maggie," Killian and Lacy said together.

I threw my hands up. I was out. Who was I to interrupt their little game of bad cop/sex cop when there was a mystery vampire on the desk?

Lacy hitched her hip and leaned over the dead vampire, looking at his face, "I don't recognize him from any of our reward posters, Maggie."

"That's the problem."

She snapped her gum. "Did you just kill a vampire that you are not supposed to be killing?"

"No, I'm pretty sure he definitely needed killing, we just need help figuring out exactly who he is and how much killing he needed."

Lacy walked over to the cabinet and got out her fang printing kit. She popped open his mouth with a pencil and made him bite down into the putty. She threw the kit into a plastic baggie and put it into a pneumatic chute. The little cylinder went flying through the glass tube up and out of the room.

"It's gonna take me a few days," she warned.

"That's cool!" I replied. "Killian and I are just getting the shop set up."

"You could deliver the results in person," Killian offered with a smile.

I could feel the room heat up from all the way over from where I was standing. I slapped Killian's shoulder. "Come on, Romeo. No glamouring The Other Side's finest."

Lacy pinched my arm. "He can glamour The Other Side's finest whenever and however long he wants, and if you two are wanting my help, I am suggesting that he pony up."

"Bribing an Other Side official is a federal offense, Lacy," I pointed out.

"I'll lose the paperwork if the government decides to press charges."

I grabbed Killian by the elbow. He was continuing to shoot out the laser rays of love from his eyes as I dragged him out of the room.

"Thank you, Lacy! So glad to know you are doing this purely out of service to your fellow man!" I shouted.

Killian shook his head as we walked down to our car. "I could be her fellow man."

"Can it, elf."

CHAPTER FOUR

I unlocked the door to MacKay & MacKay Tracking and ushered Killian in. The office hadn't been touched in a week and still smelled a little like werewolves and vampires. I made note to pick up some Undead Strength Febreeze the next time I was at the store.

I flipped on the light and opened up the window to get some air moving through the place. Killian walked over to my dad's desk and was just about to sit down.

"Wait!" I said.

He froze midway down.

I grabbed a chair and put it on The Other Side of my desk. "Why don't you sit here today?"

Killian looked at the chair and looked at me. He calmly stood, walked over, and sat. He looked at me with those great baby blues and nailed me with some truth. "You did not want me sitting at your father's desk, did you?"

I shifted uncomfortably.

"If we are to go into business, the day will come when I will need a place to sit, Maggie, and it makes sense that it should be at a desk which is not currently being used."

"Yeah, well..."

He stared at me. He had this habit of waiting patiently for me to finish perfectly unfinishable sentences.

"...yeah," I finished, lamely.

"Let me know if you are having second thoughts about our partnership arrangement."

"No!" I said, shutting him down. "No, that's not it at all. It's just... let me just clean out the drawers and stuff first."

Killian gave me a smile, totally knowing all the stuff I wasn't saying about how tough it was going to be to look at a desk where my dad had sat for the past twenty years and to see another face. The fact he didn't make me say it was pretty much proof positive I couldn't have asked for a better partner than this damned elf. Instead, he just said, "Take all the time you need."

He looked around as I grabbed a box and started emptying things. "So, what do you two do all day?"

"Oh, we usually just wait for someone to call."

"You sit here, waiting? For clients to find you?" Killian asked with, dare I say, some incredulity in his voice.

"Hey! It works, hot shot. Don't go dissing the system before you have a chance to give it a shake."

The phone rang.

"See?" I said, pointing at the phone. "It's like kismet. It's like people know that we are here and they need us." I picked up the phone, listened for a moment, and then hung up. "Telemarketer."

Killian motioned around the room. "If this is your typical day, might I suggest a receptionist and working from home?"

"That's not the way these things work, Killian. They just know when we're here. Plus, some of our clients don't even have fingers to dial."

"You are frightening me, Maggie."

"That's why we have to be here. In case they come through the door."

"How do they come through the door if they do not have fingers to turn the knob?"

"They bash it down."

"What?"

"And so we also have to be here to put the door back on the hinges."

"How often do you have those sorts of clients?"

"...often...?" I admitted.

Killian looked really uncomfortable and started to get up. "I believe, Maggie, I might call it a day—"

The phone rang. I pointed at Killian. "You see, doubter? What did I tell you? It's like magic!"

He held up his hands, motioning to me to prove him wrong.

"Hello?" I asked as I picked up the receiver. I grabbed a pen and some paper. "Really? Huh. All right. We'll be right over." I hung up. "Crap."

"Who was it?" he asked.

"General manager of the Empress Adelaide. Evidently, they are having a bit of a ghost problem." I shook my head. "We should have worked from home."

CHAPTER FIVE

I couldn't believe we were in the same place twice in one week, albeit a pretty nice place to be twice in one week.   But, the fact we were here meant that something was definitely going on, you know, other than our own little run-in with haunted soap dispensers and mystery vampires.   Needless to say, the prospect of more toilet-adjacent undead thrilled me to no end. At least, this time, I got to wear pants.

"Maggie, just think, all-you-can-eat waffles twice in one week!" Killian tried to cheer me as we parked.

"Sorry, I was distracted by the All-You-Can-Read-Death-Threats in the bathroom sink."

"Our new employer did not say what this was about?"

"Nope.   Just that they had illuminated the bat signal in the sky and our presence was requested."

"What is a bat signal? Does it relate to vampires?"

"First off, I can't believe you don't know that reference, and second off, let's hope not.   Did you pack your bag?"

He patted the sack sitting upon his lap. "I hear they have an indoor swimming pool. How remarkably human! We heard of such things in our human studies class. Imagine it! A pool of water inside a boat which is sitting upon the water. It is such a strange order to things."

"Not so strange," I replied.

"Did the passengers think that if they kept the pool inside, they would not get wet if it rains?"

"Okay, so maybe a little strange."

"I just wonder what other sort of oddities we might come across."

"Probably not many."

"I wonder if I should write a paper about the early 20th-century habits of the water-faring humans for an advanced degree program," he mused as he got out and looked excitedly at the boat.

"Your nerd is showing, Killian."

"Pardon?" he asked, looking to see if something was hanging out that shouldn't.

I patted him on the shoulder. "Save your money, elf. What we do doesn't require an education."

"You are merely being modest, Maggie. You have exhibited a great understanding of society and cultures."

"Merely the byproduct of trying to stay alive," I replied, locking the door and pocketing my keys. "You ready for this?"

"I look forward to enjoying a cruise for two with you."

I rolled my eyes.

We walked over to the little office area next to the hotel check-in. A phone call was placed and then we were whisked away and deposited in a tiny office on one of the middle floors. It was a nicely appointed room. Paneled walls, mid-century modern chairs and desk in the middle of the room. The orange industrial carpet probably wasn't the best choice, but it sort of worked in a poor man's decor sort of way.

The manager, one Julio Tiron, entered. He was a little guy. Latino with a bushy brown mustache and a bald pate. He was a ball of pent up energy, twitchy, and someone who should probably cut back a little on the coffee. He seemed like he was counting the minutes until this could be over and he could move on to the next crisis. He waved his hand to indicate that we should sit in the chairs across from him. We sat.

Julio wiped the sweat from him head and opened up a color-coded red folder. "I am glad that you were able to finally get here. You came highly recommended from Father Killarney."

I swear to God, that priest had the hookups. Dollars-to-donuts, it wasn't from bingo night.

"We're having a ghost problem," he began.

I pulled out my notebook. "What are you seeing? Ghosts? Poltergeist? Removal systems are slightly different for each one."

"No! No!" he said, holding up his hands and stopping me right there. "I don't want you to remove them. They're missing. I want you to find them and bring them back."

I lowered my notebook and looked over at Killian for confirmation we had heard the same thing before asking, "What?"

The manager explained, "Ghosts are completely welcome here on the Empress Adelaide. We welcome them in with open arms. We WANT them to stay and make themselves comfortable. We prefer it when they are our noisy neighbors." He pulled a brochure out from inside his desk. It had scary pictures of the boat in fog and dramatic lighting. "This is a haunted boat. We maintain a very exclusive clientele that stays in our hotel strictly for the experience of having an encounter with a ghost, and I have some very underwhelmed clients at this point. Word is getting out all over the message boards that things are completely ordinary here. This is a problem. Someone is either scaring them away or crossing them over and I need you to find out who and stop them. Whatever is going on is ruining my business."

I suddenly realized why Mom wasn't here. It was her life mission to calm down cranky ghosts and here this guy wanted us to stir up the mess.

"Um... I have never been asked to do anything like this before. Usually people want the ghosts to go away..." I mentioned off-handedly. Killian kicked me. The look on his face seemed to say 'quit scaring away the man who wants to give us money.'

"Well, I'm sure you'll adapt." Julio pulled out an envelope with two room keys inside. "I have taken it upon myself to reserve you both a stateroom."

"Separate beds," Killian and I said at the same time.

"Yes, separate beds," he continued, looking a little annoyed that we were talking when he was outlining his master plan to us. "I would have given you separate rooms but I can't afford to comp two rooms in this economy. You charge by the hour, correct?"

I nodded.

"Well, work fast. You have 48 hours and then I move on to someone who knows what they are doing. If you don't figure out a solution, I am only paying you half your rate."

I looked at my partner and he looked at me, "Um... that's not how we operate..."

"Well, that is how you will need to operate if you want this job. Think of it as a working vacation."

I so wanted to just grab this guy by the back of the neck and give him a hands-on demonstration of my idea of a working vacation, but we needed the money. Killian shrugged. I shrugged. I guess we were both on board, so to speak, whether we wanted to or not.

"Okay, but if we win, you double our salary."

The manager looked at me crossly. "That was not a part of our deal."

"We don't have a deal, we just have your demands. So, if we are going to risk not getting our salary for failure, you get to carry the risk of our success."

He sat there for a moment, then reached out his hand. "Deal."

CHAPTER SIX

We checked into our room. There were two tiny twin beds on either side of the tiny space. Little portholes looked out onto the lights of Long Beach. I threw my bag on my bed and Killian perched gently on his. This was the first time we spent a hotel stay with each other that didn't involve imminent death. Yet. What a change.

I opened up my bag and started unwadding my clothes. I made sure everything I owned was wad-and-wear. Life is too short to fold.

Killian, on the other hand, had every single gawddamned pair of tights folded into neat little squares inside of his round little knapsack. I'm pretty sure I wouldn't last a minute in his elfin forest.

I kicked the boots off my feet and threw myself onto the bed. "So, nap for thirty minutes before our adventures begin?"

"Or, perhaps we do not sleep on our employer's dime and start immediately, so that we do not risk losing half of our salary for failure."

I fluffed the pillow. "Oh, come on Killian. Do I detect a hint of doubt in your voice? We'll have this thing solved before the boat whistle blows midnight."

"I am not inclined to share your enthusiasm."

"Nothing was ever solved with false modesty."

"The success ratio with false bravado is about the same."

Something was bugging him. I propped myself up on my elbow. "What's the deal?"

Killian sat down on the other bed and explained it very slowly to me so that I could keep up. "You do not hear ghosts. I do not hear ghosts. It would appear that our one entry point of information is, therefore, blocked."

I shrugged. "Like you heard the man say, there aren't any ghosts to talk to."

"I still wonder why you, specifically, were called in."

"Probably because my mom wouldn't be caught dead taking this sort of case."

"Maggie, there are mediums and ghost hunters all over America that would be better suited for engaging with these beings and discovering what the problem was. Why hire someone who is unable to hear what your key witnesses have to say?"

"What are YOU trying to say, Killian, because I'm pretty sure I'm unable to hear what you're getting at."

He threw up his hands. "I am attempting to point out to you that there is more than meets the eye on this case. Something is affecting the ghosts at the same time we discovered a vampire in a bathroom in the middle of the day. I think our employer knows there is more going on here than a medium would be able to handle and the sooner we guard ourselves against this unknown, preferably before darkness falls, the better our chances of survival will be."

I patted Killian's arm. "There, there, partner. No one in this business is going to go around getting themselves killed while I am co-owner."

"It is not me that I am worried about."

Killian obviously needed to noodle through some ideas on his own with me out of yelling distance so I sat up and said, "I'm going to get some caffeine, since obviously sleep isn't going to be the thing allowing me to stay up late tonight."

Killian shook his head.

"I'll get one for you, too," I offered. "It ain't nectar, but maybe a little sugar in your system will make you less of a brat."

"I hope the machine devours your gold pieces," he said.

"Brat."

I wandered out into the hall and found the vending area. The guy ahead of me pushed the Coke button and out tumbled his can. I put my dollar in and pressed the same button and out came a Pepsi.

I sighed and stuck in another dollar.

Out came another Pepsi.

There was someone behind me and I let them go ahead as I rummaged through my pockets for more change. They hit Coke and got what they wanted.

I found another buck and pressed the button. Out came another damned Pepsi.

A face suddenly appeared in the shiny glass of the vending machine. I sprang back, clutching my heart. You know, they say that phobias are always rooted in some sort of negative experience and I gotta say, as I watched that ghost silently laugh I remembered why I hated them so much.

"Are you fucking kidding me?!?! A haunted Coke machine that only serves Pepsi?!?" I looked closer and then the face disappeared. "The moment I get a chance, I'm dooming you to an eternity haunting the deep fryer at McDonalds!"

I shook my head and wandered back to the room. I pushed open the door.

"Well, I had my first encounter," I said as I dumped all the beverages on the bathroom counter. "Seems this place isn't as deserted as el jefe would be inclined to let us believe."

Killian didn't say anything, which was not like him. I peered around the corner into the bed area to see if he still had his tights in a twist.

Fucking elf.

Killian, damn his dainty little ears, was fast asleep. I picked up the end of his mattress and dumped him on the floor.

"What the fuck???" I shouted at him.

Killian rubbed his eyes, "What?"

"What the hell are you doing sleeping???"

Killian looked at me like I was going crazy. "You indicated you would be happiest if we took a nap, so I decided you were much more knowledgeable on such matters and I should listen to your recommendations."

"That is not how you let me win!" I shouted. "You let me win by letting me going to sleep."

"But you were not here," he explained, looking very confused.

"Exactly. Because I was out in the hall trying to get you a Coke and was only able to get you a Pepsi!"

Killian was not following. "That... too... would also be agreeable."

"No! You're not following what I'm saying!"

"I believe you are correct..." he said slowly as if he was waiting for me to jump down his throat. I have no idea why.

"The vending machine is haunted."

He started to laugh. "I find that highly improbable."

"It kept giving me Pepsis."

"Perhaps it was merely a stocking error."

"And then I saw the face of a ghost in the vending machine."

"That would indicate perhaps it is more than a stocking error."

"That's what I've been trying to tell you." I threw Killian's boots at him. "Up. Get up. You win. We have ghosts to catch."

CHAPTER SEVEN

We stood on the upper deck next to the little sign that said "Ghost Tour."

Killian leaned over, "Did admission come in our welcome packet?"

"Don't worry. I'm expensing it."

"Why the tour?" he asked. "Would it not be better to begin our investigation ourselves rather than with a large group of humans?"

"Figure if we have folks to hunt down which neither you nor I can hear or feel, sometimes it's a good idea to ask the locals if they have any leads on where they hang out. Also, if our job is to bring the ghosts back, I need to know where to dump them."

"By the way, how do we plan on gathering up these ghosts?" Killian asked.

"Haven't quite worked out that bit, yet," I shrugged.

"Perhaps we can just ask them nicely," Killian suggested.

"I don't understand the words coming out of

your mouth."

Killian stepped aside as a large family of five joined the queue.

"It would be so much easier if they came swarming around naked throats like vampires or something," I said. "But ghosts need a sloppy death and I REALLY don't want to resort to killing passengers all so our boss gets his quota of dead people." As the family behind us jostled me, I continued the thought, "Although I could be persuaded."

"We would need to charge extra for that."

I sighed. "Right? Not at these rates."

Our tour guide lifted the velvet rope and ourselves along with fifteen other giggling tourists made our way into the bowels of the boat.

We stood at the back of the tour as we came to a stop at the base of a stairway. Rows of staterooms lined the hall. Our tubby Irish tour guide was sweating his way through his spiel. His pits had the stain of too many steps walked and not enough time spent next to the air vents.

Someone's baby was losing its cool and would not stop wailing.

I leaned over to Killian and whispered, "Hate to be the one with a room next to that family."

Killian sighed. "When is your sister's due date?"

"Not for a long, long time."

The tour guide wiped his brow and pointed to a plaque on the side of a large picture of the boat. Rattling off the canned text of his spiel, he said, "This is the door to the first class playroom. It is currently a storage closet. But there have been reports of hearing a baby cry. In fact just last week, someone stayed behind to take pictures and reported hearing it.

Moving on." With as much excitement as a Monday morning, the tour guide motioned for the group to follow him as he walked away.

I grabbed Killian's arm and held him back for a minute as all of the tourists snapped pictures of the nondescript door, totally missing the fact the psychic activity they were looking for was happening in front of them. "You heard that too, right?"

He nodded, staring intently at the door as if he was trying to memorize everything that was going on in this moment. "Indeed, I did."

"Well," I sighed. "That's just fantastic."

Killian gave me a sideways glance. "I would think that this was, indeed, a fantastic lead. We have one less ghost to track down for our employer."

I realized the group was getting way ahead of us, so Killian and I jogged to catch up. The tour guide was unlocking the door to a stateroom and saying that the ghost that inhabited this room would pull off your covers in the middle of the night and pinch your butt. Sounded like some dates I had been on.

Our guide was a little too big to fit into the room with all of us, so he just motioned us through. "This is the most psychically active room onboard and we can no longer use it as a rentable room due to the number of complaints from our guests of haunted activity. Look around and I'll meet you here when you are finished."

"I would think that a haunted room would actually be a selling point if our employer is hoping to gain the reputation as a haunted site," Killian murmured.

"Very 'actually', unless bad things happened to the people who made the mistake of sleeping in here," I replied. "Wonder how bad it was?"

The room was stripped bare with nothing but a bunch of broken furniture all over the place.

Killian inspected the cracked porthole glass. "I would hazard a guess it was fairly bad."

"Poltergeists. I can't believe they want us to try and figure out how to keep poltergeists onsite. Most folks pay good money to get these cleaned up."

"If you were to describe the differences between a ghost and a poltergeist...?" Killian offhandedly asked.

"Ghosts just lurk around and are annoying. Poltergeists can move things."

"Like soap and cans of soda?"

"Oh, now, look who is starting to understand what I was saying about the damned soda cans. Next time I tell you about a haunted vending machine—"

"I am heartily sorry."

"Damned right you are."

"Do you need me to apologize one more time, or are you ready to continue?"

"Just once more."

"I am sorry."

"Excellent." We shook on it.

The tour group was losing its mind over all the broken things.

"Earth humans are strange creatures," Killian muttered, shaking his head at a shattered marble bedside table.

The bathroom lights flickered on and off.

"What the hell?" I said, jumping. Have I mentioned how much I hate ghosts?

"It is most likely an electrical surge," Killian reassured me, trying to calm me down.

"Right," I replied, eyeing the bulb suspiciously.

All of the tourists started taking flash pictures,

which sort of defeated capturing the lights flickering on and off.

"Perhaps it is only a trick to make people feel like they are experiencing supernatural powers," Killian suggested.

"Or it is only poltergeists," I said.

"Or poltergeists."

"Don't agree with me, elf."

I elbowed my way out. I had seen what I needed to see and didn't need to spend another minute in that room. Killian followed me out.

He gave me a little sideways squeeze. "Never fear, Maggie. I shall protect you from these creatures of your darkest fears."

Some girls like a man around the house to squish spiders. Me, I found nothing as attractive as a guy willing to squash dead things. But Killian was missing the point. "I will not turn be turning down your offer to go after these ghosts whenever they do show up, but I think we've got a bigger issue here."

"That being?"

"Think of the ghosts as a nice little gathering of bacteria. You kill off the nice bacteria and only the strongest, meanest bacteria survive and they start to infest the place. Pretty soon you have a nasty colony of resistant bacteria that are going to make some people very, very sick."

Killian nodded, finally starting to get where I was going. "Something wiped out the ghosts, and so only the strong..."

"...est..."

"...strongest..."

"...harmful..."

"...strongest, harmful ghosts remain."

"You got it."

"Again, I would point out that our employer does not seem the discerning type and would rather have the dramatics of a stronger ghost than the wisps of the more benign entities."

"When did you turn all mercenary on me, Killian?"

"When I became half-partner in the financial success of this tracking business," he replied.

"Listen, what Julio wants or doesn't want doesn't change the fact that something powerful came through and wiped out the 'nice' ghosts. And when something big and powerful comes through and does an extermination like this, it usually means something mean and nasty from The Other Side is hanging out where it should not be hanging out."

"Which means more paying work for you and I?"

"Yes," I said. "But for once, could you not think about a paycheck?"

"Will Lacy be delivering the paycheck?"

"For once, could you not think about Lacy?"

"I usually think about Lacy far more than once."

I pulled out my phone. There were no messages. There was also no reception, but that was beside the point. "I wish she would call already with the results of that vampire we dropped off."

"You think the vampire has something to do with these poltergeists?"

"You think it doesn't?"

"It could be coincidence."

"I'm not going to chalk it up to nothing until we find out it's nothing."

"We can always refuse this job, Maggie," Killian pointed out. "We could enjoy the weekend in our stateroom, watch Earth television, and collect the half fee in a few days."

That actually sounded really nice, but if there was something here, I had a feeling they weren't the type to let us sit in our room eating bon-bons. As Dad always used to say, "Err on the side of kick-butt before your butt is kicked."

"I'll be fine," I said. "I just prefer something I can stake over things that go bump in the night."

The rest of the tour group had exited the room and were excitedly showing off their pictures, exclaiming to each other that they had most definitely had a close encounter of the Other Worldly kind because their flash had lit up some dust in the air. They had absolutely no idea that when you encounter a ghost, there is no mistaking it for dust.

The guide led us down the hallway and down a couple of flights of stairs, right into the center of the ship. He announced, "We are now entering the most haunted swimming pool on our ship."

I felt like this was akin to saying, "You're my favorite oldest daughter," but who was I to quibble?

The guide was still talking about the features of the room, the diving boards, the mother-of-pearl ceiling, the tile work. When he finally let us in, it was actually a really pretty room. It was two stories, the one with the pool and deck, then a sweeping staircase that led to a balcony that wrapped around the whole pool. The better for industrious young'uns to look down unsuspecting tops. There were empty His and Hers dressing rooms at both the front and back of the room.

"This is the site of the most haunted area on our ship. We have had paranormal investigators come by and they suggest there is a vortex located inside the

dressing room over to your right," he said in his
bored-spiel voice. "Please feel free to look around
the room on your own."

Killian jerked his head towards the corner and we
both wandered over to this supposed vortex.

It was a fucking portal alright. It was closed right
now, but I could feel the signature. It's like scar tissue
on the boundary. Run your hand across the surface
and you can feel a walker's efforts.

"We got a weak spot right here, Killian," I said,
pointing out the rip, forgetting for a moment I wasn't
working with my dad.

He stared at it intently. "I do not see a thing."

It was just a little moment, but one of those
punch-to-the-gut reality checks. It wasn't the elf's
fault. I just hadn't quite been ready. I... wasn't
working with my dad. I took a breath and squished
all those feelings down before Killian got a whiff of
them. "The boundary is naturally thin here, but it also
has a scar in it. If you open up a portal once or twice,
it can heal itself so that you never even know a portal
was even there. But I can feel this one like a keloid,
which means it is opened often by someone who
doesn't really know what they're doing. Someone's
been moving things in and out of this pool room and
it wasn't too long ago."

"If you all would follow me, please," the tour guide
asked. "We need to keep moving along."

I whispered to Killian, "First chance we have to
ditch them, you and I come back here."

That's when I saw her. A little girl walking slowly
along the upper level. She was dressed in a lacy white
dress with a drop waist and her blonde hair hung in
curls that would have sent Shirley Temple into fits of

jealous rage. The little girl looked down at me and stared straight into my eyes. I put my hand on Killian's arm and pointed. He looked up at her and she vanished.

"Did you see that?"

He nodded.

"She was completely corporeal. We are way in over our heads, Killian."

"Perhaps we should reconsider my suggestion to take the half payment and enjoy our vacation," he offered.

I looked around at the milling tourists. They were so desperate for a ghostly encounter and had completely missed that there was one standing right above them.

"No," I said. "That little kid specifically wanted us to see her. She hid herself from everyone else. I can't leave her roaming this boat when she's asking for help."

I might not have my mom's gifts, but I had picked up a thing or two about the family trade. Being a ghost sucks balls. If you miss that window into the afterworld, you are in for a world of misery for the rest of eternity. It is how my mom tried to teach me to have a little more sympathy for the ghost banging around our place when I was a kid. So, if this little girl was stuck, and she knew enough that I might be able to give her a hand... well. Sometimes you're in a place for a reason.

"Maggie, are you getting soft on me?"

"Don't go spreading it around," I warned.

Killian and I dutifully shuffled along with the herd as our group was led out and into an elevator. The guide pressed the button for "down." Down, down,

down into the bowels of this ship until we couldn't go any farther without diving gear. We stepped out into the hull of the boat. As far as the eye could see was a rusty room with open beams and catwalks. The ceiling seemed like it was a million miles above us, which it might as well have been—the guide announced that we were thirty feet below the waterline and only six inches of steel was protecting us from the crush of the ocean.

There was a catwalk way up there, though, and the tour guide pointed up. "People have reported seeing a ghost-like figure overhead, to hear troops marching around when there aren't soldiers on this ship."

That was all well and good, pretty typical Haunted Wherever script. I always felt like invoking "troops" was a way to stir patriotic feelings or gain sympathy from the crowd. I was so busy judging the tour guide for playing his tourists that I didn't notice the gaping hole in the middle of the bulkhead until I was almost in it. It was... massive. Just... a hole... in the steel plating separating one section of the boat from another. Physically, probably thirty-by-thirty feet, but crackling with energy along its edges. I looked at Killian, "Do you feel that?"

He shook his head.

"What are you even good for?" I asked.

"Looking good while saving you."

"Touché. There is an energy signature around this whole... hole," I said, pointing at the big opening in front of us. "There are fissures in the boundary. It's like someone has been digging a tunnel with a teaspoon so no one will notice while they get ready to bust on through. This is massive and SO not legal."

Killian gave a low whistle. "So, do we return to

The Other Side to report it?"

"They'll just send me back to fix it," I said, wishing my cell phone could take a picture of Other Worldly Energy so that I could send it to my dad.

"Would they pay you to come back and fix it?"

"I'm getting the feeling we don't have time to wait for the bureaucratic bullshit machine to spit out the right paperwork. I'll send a report as soon as we get into cell territory, but I'm feeling like this one might be gratis. You know. If we don't all die."

"Die?" Killian repeated, suddenly realizing the gravity of our sitch.

I stared at the cracks in the boundary with a sinking feeling that made the Titanic look like it had just taken on a little extra water. "Killian, what did we get ourselves into?"

The tour guide was rounding everyone else back up.

Killian adjusted his shirt with the stoicism of a soldier going into battle. "Well, let us find out."

I sighed, "After you."

We walked out of the cavernous hull by going up some stairs and through the kind of door you would expect to see inside a submarine. Inside was the engine room. It was a maze of white tubes, narrow metal walkways, and pipes. The tour guide stopped us by a door marked with "13".

Our guide got very quiet: "A young sailor was trapped in this water-tight door, crushed to death when it closed during a drill. People report seeing his ghost wandering the engine room. He haunts these passages and leaves his mark, a three-fingered oil smear, on people's cheeks and legs."

The tour guide pointed at an escalator at the end

of the room which would take everyone upstairs to a nice little museum with exhibits of the ship. But while his back was turned, I saw who it was leaving the oil marks on people's legs. His spindly little hand reached over the catwalk.

It was a gargoyle. They look just like the ones you see on the cornices of church buildings because... well... those are gargoyles. They hang out on buildings during the day, come to life at night. There is a work/study program that The Other Side runs on the smaller buildings, but if you hang out on Earth long enough, you can get yourself promoted all the way up to Notre Dame, which has need of as many gargoyles as they can manage, let me tell you.

I had no idea what this guy was doing down here on a ship, though.

The tour made its way upstairs, chatting and showing off their pictures to one another. I grabbed Killian's arm and held him back.

"I want to go back to that swimming pool," I announced loudly, hoping the gargoyle wouldn't catch on that I was about to find out what the hell was going on.

"I am on board with this plan," said Killian.

As we walked past one of the engines, I caught the gargoyle's shadow behind one of the pumps.

I made the sign of the cross. "Oh Father in Heaven, I ask for your protection and deliverance," I prayed.

The gargoyle froze and turned towards me like a great big hand had reached up and grabbed his head.

I called out, "I see you, I know what you are, and I think we probably need to have a little chat."

The gargoyle sighed and relaxed, coming out into

view. He was a little guy, more like a gargoyle that you would find sitting on a bookshelf than on the cornice of a cathedral, but suitably gargoyle-scary. He gave me a taste of his little roar as he admonished me, "Better be careful calling out those sorts of words. Crying wolf'll make us stop paying attention to you."

"I'm usually able to handle the wolves on my own," I replied, leaning against the railing. "Funny to run into one of your kind here."

"Funny to run into you, Tracker Maggie," he replied.

"Funny that you know my name," I stated, suddenly on guard.

"Friend of Killarney."

Was there anything on this boat that wasn't buddies with our priest? "That figures."

"He is the current caretaker of my childhood home," the gargoyle explained.

"Childhood home?"

"His church on La Brea."

"So how do you get from a church on La Brea to a 1930's ocean liner?" I asked.

"There's a chapel onboard."

I oh-so-helpfully pointed out, "You're in the engine room, gargoyle..."

"The name is George," he corrected me.

"Okay, GEORGE, you're in the engine room. I don't see a chapel around here."

"It's topside, but there are too many tourists with a Sharpie pen. You wake up once with a gang tag drawn across your forehead and you decide to do your protecting from a safer spot."

"Fair enough, but the sun is up. Shouldn't you be pretending to be concrete or something?"

"The sun isn't up anymore, Maggie," he replied.

I looked down at my watch. It was seven o'clock and sure enough, dark had settled and I didn't even know it. Great. "Okay, so I totally missed seeing the sunset from a porthole window. So, you still didn't answer my question. What's a gargoyle like you doing hanging out in an engine room like this?"

He pointed to a little retro sign that most folks would mistake for adorable days-gone-by advertisement. It read "Gargoyle Oil."

I looked at him. "Unless Earth suddenly started making oil from gargoyles, this is an Other Side brand, isn't it?"

He laughed and hopped across a couple of beams, "We've been the official caretakers of the Ghost Spirit since 1934. Gargoyle Oil. Nothing better for lubing your parts."

Killian smiled at me.

"Shut up." I turned to George. "So why is an Earth vessel using an Other Side product?"

"You're an idiot, Tracker Maggie. The name Gray Ghost doesn't refer to her paint. This entire ship is a ghost. It rides between dimensions. You get in the right space, and you can walk right into the underworld. Been my job to keep the evil spirits away since 1934."

This was news to me. "The entire ship is a ghost?"

"Yep."

"I knew I hated this place," I muttered to Killian.

He put a hand on my arm to keep me on task and asked George, "You said that you have been tasked with battling evil spirits. Do you know why the more docile ghosts are disappearing?"

"Vampires," he replied matter-of-factly.

I hooked my thumb at Killian and myself. "Since you mentioned it, we caught one in the men's bathroom last weekend."

"Only one? Having you on board is probably scattering them like cockroaches under a kitchen light. This boat has always been a portal for vampires. What do you think that vortex is?"

"The vortex in the swimming pool?" I asked.

He nodded.

"I have no idea."

"Maggie, half of this boat has rooms with no windows, passageways with no light, plus they have to make the food here for tourist palates that don't like a lot of spice. You won't find an ounce of garlic on anything outside the Italian dressing on their salads. It is perfect for their kind."

But it was slowly starting to dawn on me. My dad and I had built a portal near the San Onofre power plant. The power fluctuations made it hard for anyone to find. You'd have to be a human lemur to jump through that thing on a lark.

And the vampires had set this one up thinking somehow I wouldn't track it down.

"How long have they been using it?" I asked.

"Since the boat was built. How do you think the vampires got from Europe to the Americas?" he asked.

"Flew?"

A rush of water came through a pipe overhead. George grabbed a wrench and made a ten-foot standing leap to tighten the bolt. He hung by one spindly little claw as he pulled, lower jaw jutting from exertion. "Not with the sun rising before they could make it across the ocean. This boat let them do it in style. And pick up passengers along the way. The Other Side is dry where the Earth's Atlantic Ocean lies. It was as close to a train that the vampires have ever had. Pop over here, walk through the portal in the swimming pool to destinations on The Other Side, pop back to Earth when they needed to keep going. It was a highly developed transportation system."

"So what is making all the ghosts disappear?" I asked.

"Vampires have been using the portal too much lately. Been sucking the ghosts into the boundary."

"Shit." I turned to Killian. "Well, I'm now starting to understand why they didn't ask my mom to take this job."

"Do you think she knew?"

"Are you kidding me? We were both here last weekend and neither of us had any clue. We're all flying blind." I turned back to the gargoyle. "So, you want to give us a hand tracking down these vampires?"

He shook his head. "No can do, Maggie. Ever since that incident with the soap—"

"The death-suds? Wait! That was me!"

"I know. Since that slipped past, I got myself a nice little reprimand and order to stick to a more manageable area. My territory extends as far as this floor. I step one foot outside those doors and there'll be a warrant on my head for you to haul me back to The Other Side before you reach the portal. It is a lose-lose."

"Um... I'll get paid. That might be a benefit."

George wasn't buying it. He gave me a wink and

scampered along the pipes like the eensy weensie spider climbing up a drain. "Wish I could help, Maggie! Watch your back!"

CHAPTER EIGHT

Between the crackling portal waiting to happen and the intel that George shared with us, this job was looking like one big bucket of fun. Killian and I were up in the museum, watching flickering footage taken on the boat back in its heyday. There weren't any seats, so I just leaned against the wall and stretched out the back of my legs, trying to pretend that I was a person who gave a crap about stretching or history.

As the movie continued, my brain started spinning with excuses for how to get out of this mess. The voice over dude was saying something about how the world's elite flocked to the Empress Adelaide for the ultimate in luxury and leisure travel. Face after face after face I recognized, and not from the Golden Years of Hollywood. If these folks were human, they would have to have had the world's best plastic surgeon. No, these were vampires. I recognized them from their rap sheets and their final moments on the end of my stake. It took a little while for the pieces to click in my brain, but they were slowly starting to work their way into place.

"This entire boat is about travel and luxury."

"Indeed, that is what the man on the film just said," replied Killian, pointing at the screen. "I assure you I was listening."

"Shut up, what I am saying is that if vampires want to move across the globe in style, someone has to be around to take their checks."

"Like the owner of the boat?"

"No, an intermediary who is going to ensure that his guests get every luxury while not eating their travel agent. He probably collects a hefty convenience fee on top of it. So, who is the biggest, richest vampire we know...?"

"Vaclav."

"Bingo. And I'm not talking about onboard entertainment."

"Vaclav is not generally one to entertain."

I tried to let it pass. I did. I tried. But I couldn't. "No, Killian, I was referring to the 'bingo' part of that sentence..."

"What is 'the bingo'?"

I sighed so hard I think I sprained a lung. First waffles, now this... Killian was missing out on so much in that elfin forest. "Bingo. It's a game with numbers... I'll take you when we get back to Los Angeles. There is a drag queen who sells tupperware while she runs the game in West Hollywood. You'll love it." I looked back at the film.

"The thing that bothers me..." mused Killian.

"What?" I asked.

"The thing that bothers me is that there are vampires still using this portal," he said.

"Yeah... I would say that is a little bothersome..." I replied.

"This boat has been in one place for the past forty years, Maggie. It was originally used to get vampires from one spot to the next. But now it is just an open door from one side to the next. What lies on The Other Side of the boundary and is waiting to cross? Was this boat placed in the same spot as a lair? And if they must construct a portal in the hold, what is so big that it cannot cross through the vortex in the swimming pool?"

"You are just a ray of sunshine, aren't you?" I said.

"Merely here to shed light upon the situation," replied Killian.

"Can't we just go live in a nice, dark cave somewhere?"

Killian shook his head.

I sighed and pointed up the stairs. "Okay, let's go check out this pool of doom and see how long it'll be before we find ourselves swimming in death up to our necks."

We traced our path back. It was late enough that the halls were pretty much cleared out from all but hotel guests. There were some folks dressed up in pretty gowns for a fancy dinner and I heard a couple of them say that there was an interactive murder-mystery show tonight. I tried not to think about the fact that if Killian and I didn't play our cards right, their show might get a bit more interactive than what they signed up for.

We kept making wrong turns looking for the pool. I was having serious trouble tracking down this vortex, and considering the fact that I was a magical tracker, all the not-tracking-down was starting to make me feel pretty frickin' freaked out. Finally, drawing on our highly advanced skills at reading signs with arrows on them, we got to the first class swimming area. Killian looked at me and I looked at him, and we both took out our weapons.

"Ready?" he asked.

"Ready," I replied, and pushed open the door.

Inside, the room was the same pool area we saw before, with its mother-of-pearl ceiling and empty swimming pool. Except it wasn't empty anymore. Instead, the pool was filled with this green glow that rippled its light off the ceiling as if it was phosphorescent water. I heard laughter and the sound of splashing. The pitter pat of tiny feet ran right across in front of me, the child's giggling followed by a woman's laughter.

I looked up at the balcony and standing above the pool was a woman dressed in a white wedding gown, holding a child's hand. The kid was dressed in blue sailor suit. Gave a whole new meaning to I'd rather be dead than caught in that get-up. I'm pretty sure no one packed these outfits in their overnight bags.

I looked at Killian to make sure I hadn't completely lost my mind. Gotta say, part of me wished this was all residual hallucinations from one-too-many dimension jumps, but no such luck. He saw it, too.

"We are sure seeing a lot of ghosts for people who shouldn't be able to see ghosts," I muttered.

An explosion of white light took over the room. It was coming from the dressing room, where I had seen the vortex earlier. The little blonde girl in the dress whom I had seen on the balcony before suddenly reappeared and was trying to shout something at Killian and me.

A woman in black emerged from the portal. This dame was movie-star gorgeous, kind of a Vivian Leigh in a flouncy 1930's gown straight out of a Busby Berkeley flick. But her swinging good looks didn't make up for what she was trying to ferry over.

Vampires. Two of them all dressed up like they were getting ready for some sort of booze cruise, complete with Hawaiian shirts and sandals with socks. I'm pretty sure this was breaking all sorts of maritime laws. If not maritime laws, fashion laws. This pool area was the perfect place for a vampire to hide out. No windows. No external light. Just sweet, sweet darkness and all you had to do was put up with a couple of nosy tourists every couple of hours.

My stake was in my hand before they were able to look around and figure out where I was.

THWACK! THWACK!

Two stakes, right through the heart.

I turned to Killian and held my hand up. I could see him trying to remember the appropriate response. I took his hand and showed him the high five.

He nodded his head, remembering. "Good job, partner."

The little girl was screaming silently and all of the ghosts were looking at her like she had lost her goddamned mind. But then they all looked at us.

Man, I would have done just about anything for my mom's gift right about now. The woman in black's gaze was enough to make me feel like someone had dumped cold water right down my back. She hissed, bared her fangs, and it all finally made sense to me.

The vampires turned a world walker.

Mind you, she was a lousy world walker, but that's probably why they had been able to convince her to become one of them and use her powers for evil. Nothing like being at the bottom of a food chain to make a girl decide she wants to be at the top of the food chain. Literally. The vamp-walker looked like she wasn't sure whether to come at us or hightail it through the portal.

That little kid had some ideas, though. She ran down the steps and dashed right out in front of the woman in black. She shouted something and the force of that silent shout was enough to make the woman take a step back. She looked right and then looked left, and then vanished, closing the portal behind her. And as soon as that portal vanished, the other ghosts vanished, too, to God only knows where. The little girl looked at me.

"Thank you," I whispered.

And then she was gone.

The only thing left as any proof that what had just happened had actually really happened were the bodies of two vampires lying poolside, right next to an ancient sign that said "Lifeguard on duty."

CHAPTER NINE

"So what you have is a vampire problem," I explained to Julio.

We were back in his office. It was almost nine o'clock and he still hadn't left for the day. Looked like the paperwork on his desk was multiplying like bunnies. Colored folders and typed labels were everywhere. He patted his sweaty pate with a Kleenex and shook his head, "Vampires? Well, clear them out and let's get this place haunted again."

"It isn't quite that simple," I explained. "There is a portal in your swimming pool's dressing room and I don't think I'm going to have much luck closing it."

He leaned forward, pointing his fat finger in my face. "If you expect to make any money at all from this deal, you'll seal it up. Are you or are you not one of the best world walkers this side of the boundary?"

Okay, he had me there.

"Listen, if there is anyone who can do it, it'll be me, but I don't know if I can do it," I explained.

"There's a rogue world walker who is going to open up anything I close."

"Well, get that world walker to stop."

"Again, not as easy as you're making it sound. And that also doesn't fix the problem that you have a massive illegal portal someone is building in the basement of your ship."

"Well, close that up, too."

"That's like asking someone to close up the Colorado River."

"Well, Hoover built that damn dam and it seems like it is doing an okay job."

"They didn't build the Hoover Dam in 48 hours."

"That's all the time you've got," he replied, going back to the stack of papers on his desk.

"I'm tripling our salary."

"WHAT!" Julio roared. That got his attention.

"And you're lucky I don't report you for maintaining an illegal portal without notifying The Other Side authorities," I threatened.

"I didn't even know it was here!" he sputtered.

"Tell that to the judge."

"This is extortion!"

"No, I've looked up extortion, and that is not the definition of it." I leaned forward. "This is tough. This is not just going to go away overnight."

"Well, then, stay as long as you need to make it stop!" he said.

"The point you're missing is that we might not be able to make it stop," Killian explained. "Please believe my partner when she says that this is a problem that may be bigger than both of us."

"I have a ghost ship to run." Julio relaxed into his chair. I could see the wheels of his mind slowly starting to crank. This was not a good thing. "Maybe I'll turn it into a vampire ship. That'll keep the tourist dollars rolling in."

"No, trust me, you don't want to do that," I said.

"And why not? Those goth kids are all over the sparkly vampires. I could hold Valentine's Day dances every day. A nice little bar for vampires and the people who want to get to know them."

"That is a terrible idea."

"People will pay a lot of money to get up close and personal. We'll hem them in one of the ballrooms with some holy relics and garlic. It'll be better than any haunted Halloween maze offered in Southern California!"

"Those haunted mazes have strict no-touch/no-kill policies! Look, this is a terrible plan."

"No, the more I think about this, the better it gets."

"You can't let folks here on Earth know that monsters are real, not if you want to live."

"Every child in America knows monsters are real. The fact I have confirmed evidence? They'll claim me as a hero!"

"You'll get yourself disappeared really quickly."

"I'll start the rumors and the internet will take care of the rest."

"That sounds like a great idea for a meme, but that's going to get a lot of people hurt. I, along with the authorities of The Other Side, can't let you do that."

"Well, then, you've got 36 hours left in your contract to shut up that portal or that's exactly what I'm going to do. You want to save humanity? You better put on your big girl pants and get to it. The time is wasting. Frankly, I don't really care if you do or don't. I'm sitting on a cash cow either way. You get to decide how people spend their money."

I looked at Killian, wondering if Julio understood that if he opened this boat up as a vampire theme park, he'd be the first item on the fun menu.

CHAPTER TEN

Killian and I walked up to the top decks of the Empress Adelaide. The lights of Long Beach twinkled in front of us. The sky was dark. I'm sure there were probably stars up there, but you can't see anything with all the light pollution.

A bunch of tourists were up on the top decks, taking pictures of each other as they pretended to fall overboard. Lovers strolled hand in hand and whispered sweet whatevers into each other's ears. Some of the lovers were real. What was freaking me out a whole lot more was that a lot of them were ghosts.

"What the hell?" I said as one of the ghost couples walked right through me. I felt like someone grabbed both my lungs and pushed all the air out of my body.

"I do not believe this is hell, Maggie."

"Maybe for you it's not."

Now, I had made my peace with ghostly types after our adventure in Ghost Town, but they still weren't my favorite. Give me something I could stake any day of the week over an uncontrollable mist that can come and flip your lights on and off while you're trying to watch TV. And now they were all around us.

I looked at Killian. "Did you see them?"

Killian was fixated upon a loud family where one boy was beating up on his kid brother every time his mom's back was turned. "I do not know which is the more terrifying."

We were about to learn.

My cell phone rang. I picked it up and said, "MacKay &... K Tracking. How can I help you?"

"Maggie! It's Lacy."

"Who is it?" asked Killian.

"Your girlfriend," I said. "Now let me find out why she's calling, okay?"

"Tell her to call me if she requires more payment for doing us that favor."

"She has been paid in full, elf."

"I am happy to increase her salary."

I rolled my eyes and turned back to the phone. "Lacy, what's up? You working the midnight shift?"

"Somebody's got to hold down the fort when things get ugly."

Kind of like how emergency rooms get really busy when the bars let out, The Other Side police station was its busiest after the sun went down.

"Listen, Lacy, we're stuck in the middle of a haunted boat and surrounded by ghosts right now..."

"We're all busy, Maggie," replied Lacy, not at all impressed. "I got back those fang prints on that guy you staked."

"Yeah?" I said as I pulled a notebook from my

jacket pocket. "Hit me."

"Vamp named Les Westerly. Last known record of him was in 1936 and then he disappeared. No paperwork saying he should be anywhere close to Long Beach, so on behalf of The Other Side's finest, we'd like to thank you for bringing in a skip who appears to have been hiding on Earth for the past eighty years. Your reward check is in the mail. And on that note, I have been told to tell you to quit staking vampires until you find out whether or not they should be staked, please."

"Consider me reprimanded."

"I can practically hear the waves of sorrow and regret in your voice."

"I can barely keep them contained," I replied dryly. "Thanks, Lacy!"

"Tell that partner of yours to come in anytime he'd like to be reprimanded."

"I gotta go, Lacy. Bad reception. Ghosts are screwing up the connection," and then I hung up.

"Ghosts were not 'screwing up the connection,' Maggie," Killian said.

"Trust me, things were getting screwy enough."

"What did she have to say?"

I pocketed my phone. "That vampire we got last weekend wasn't supposed to be here."

"Good!" replied Killian. "That should make the paperwork process smoother."

"Yeah, good that we didn't stake an innocent vamp. Not good that the last anyone ever saw him was eighty years ago and suddenly he appears out of nowhere in a bathroom stall dressed like he should be in The Great Gatsby. Or more to the point," I said as I pointed at all of the ghosts around us, "like he should be hanging out with these guys instead of hanging out with us."

"What do you think is going on, Maggie?"

I tried feeling the boundary, but was getting nothing. "Mom felt nothing. I'm feeling nothing. These guys shouldn't be here at all. And yet, here they are. I'm wondering if that portal downstairs is so loud, it is just drowning everything out. Sort of like noise-canceling headsets."

It was at that moment that there was the sound of a low horn. It was like a foghorn, except louder. Way louder. Earth-trembling louder. It made the entire floor rumble. And that's when I felt the shift. It wasn't just a little shift, I felt the entire boat shift. Smoke started pouring out of one of the stacks and it began glowing bright red against the night sky.

"What is that?" I asked Killian, pointing to the day-glo light coming off the top of the ship. It was like the entire place had been put under some deadhead's black light, and we were joining a party already in-progress.

He had no answers for me and was looking just as blown away as I was from the whole thing. That's when I realized what had happened. Everything beyond the boat had disappeared. The topography was the same, but the skyscrapers and touristy harbor were gone. Inside the boat, everything had a fresh new gleam to it, like it had just been built. All the ghosts had been replaced by real people strolling along the decks, and the real people were now ghosts. Porters and cruise directors walked along to make sure everyone was safe and sound. Laughter tinkled from below decks as well as the sound of an orchestra playing a swinging tune. No one seemed to notice anything was wackadoo except for me and Killian.

"Fuck."

Killian let out a slow whistle, "I should say so."

I grabbed Killian and dragged him away.

"Where are you taking me, Maggie?"

"We sort of stick out like sore thumbs," I replied, pointing down at what we were wearing and the strange looks we were getting from the passengers. Killian, in his navy blue turtleneck and slacks could probably have passed as a sailor, but me in my leathers, boots, utility belt of weapons, and neck guard were not going to be fooling anyone. I pulled Killian into a doorway and tried to pretend like we could disappear into the shadows.

Killian breathed deep. "Right. First order of business, find ourselves clothing appropriate to the local color."

"First order of business, we get back to our own time and figure out what the hell is going on," I muttered as I started feeling the air around us. "I should have told Julio to take this job and blow it out his porthole."

"What are you doing, Maggie?"

"Trying to find the weak spot."

"What do you mean?"

"To get us home."

"How do you propose to do that?"

"I'll just punch a hole in dimensions," I said as I gave Killian a good-natured punch in the arm, trying to reassure him I had everything under control. "Do you remember who you're talking to?"

"I know very well who I am talking to, Maggie."

I laced my fingers and gave my knuckles a good cracking. I rolled my head and loosened up my shoulders. I gathered up the energy and reached out to punch through dimensions... and my hand stayed exactly in this dimension.

"What the what?!?" I asked. I pushed again. Nothing. Flop sweat started prickling on my lip. "Come on!" I grunted.

Killian folded his arms and looked at me, "Whom was I talking to again?"

"I don't need any of your attitude, elf. Why isn't this working?"

"Perhaps because you are attempting to walk through both time and space?" Killian oh-so-helpfully pointed out.

Smart ass. "Excuse me, I will have you know that I completely took time into my space calculations."

"And yet, here we still are."

"How many portals to other dimensions have you opened recently, Killian? I think the answer would be none."

"Might I suggest we go down to the swimming pool instead?"

"The swimming pool...?" I repeated, trying again to bust through the dimensions.

"I seem to recollect, Maggie," he explained like I was some idiot child, "there was a natural vortex in the swimming area, which you believed was a doorway between the dimensions."

Color me an idiot.

"Good thinking. Let's see if we can remember where it is."

"And you call yourself a tracker," he said affectionately. "Come along, Maggie. Follow me."

We began walking swiftly along the deck towards a door that would most likely take us somewhere close to a door that went inside and down. That was about as close as I could remember about that pool's direction. Again, I felt like I was flying blind. Direction was completely confounding my mind.

"Why can't I remember where anything is on this ship, Killian?"

He patted my shoulder bracingly. "If there are a number of dimensions here, especially dimensions which fold upon themselves in time and space, you are probably sensing thousands of doorways and paths."

The elf made sense. I think Killian clued in on how freaked out I was, flying so blind, because he paused for a moment to reassure me. "I have traveled the elfin forest in the dead of a moonless night with nothing to guide me and I made it through. I might not be a world walker like your father, but perhaps being blind to the dimensions here shall be useful. Let me navigate us and trust I shall not let you come to harm."

I gripped Killian's hand for just a second. I didn't want to get too mushy on him, but there was a part of me that just wanted to let him know, just for a moment, that I was really grateful. "Cool," I said. "Whatever."

"So," he continued, completely letting it pass without embarrassing me, "do you believe we have traveled to a ghost dimension or just another dimension of reality?"

JUST another dimension of reality... I love how he made it sound as exciting as picking between white and wheat bread at the grocery store. As we passed another group of Depression- era people, along with some ghosties of the 21st Century to come, I said, "It doesn't feel like it's just ghosts, Killian. We know that these modern people are real people from our own world. We're stuck in some sort of other time." I stopped in my tracks. "That's why my mom can't sense them. They're not dead."

Killian put his arm behind me and moved me along. "Then it should be easier to return to our time, should it not?"

Killian and I turned the corner on the steps, then walked through a small lobby to get to the next set of stairs. That's when a bouncy little head of familiar blonde hair came running at us. Up until this point, we had been getting some funny looks, but folks were giving us a pretty wide berth. This kid, however, was coming straight at us like she recognized us. What was scarier was that both Killian and I recognized her, too. She was our little pool protector, our little badass. I didn't know whether to hug her or run. She reached us before I could decide.

Shyly, she whispered, "You're real, aren't you? Everyone said you were my imaginary friends and made fun of me, but you're really real!"

"We're real," I replied. "Here. Punch him in the gut."

Killian smacked me in the arm.

"I am Jackie," she said.

"We saw you in the pool," I said. "You yelled at a woman in black." I put up my hands. "Wait a minute. Are you the ghost who wrote in the soap bubbles and was messing around with the soda machine?"

The kid heard something behind her. Her eyes got as big as mine did the first time I found out there really was a monster under my bed. "You must help us!" she said, suddenly hyperventilating.

I slowed that kid's roll. "I know! That's what we're going to try and do."

She looked over her shoulder in fear, "She's coming. I must go!"

"Who is coming?"

"Her!"

"Tell us what you need!" I said.

"Watch out!" she warned us. "There is death all around us!"

Jackie began shaking. She pointed down the promenade. "There she is. There she is with her friends! They keep killing everyone. People go with them and then we find them with two bite-holes in their neck, and then they are like ghosts. And you can't do anything to stop them. They just want to bite you."

Killian and I looked where she was pointing and there was that gal in black with a couple of swells on her arm, the same lady who had oh-so-kindly been the cruise director to those vampires I had staked earlier.

Only I didn't think she had me and Killian on her day's events list.

The woman in black looked up, saw us, and took off the other direction. If her fangs hadn't given her away, her speed sure did. No woman should be able to run that fast in high heels. Her fellas followed after without even breaking a sweat.

It was on. Killian and I broke out in a flat sprint, getting some none-too-friendly looks from the staff. Guess they weren't used to seeing a girl in leather.

"Costumed performers coming through!" I shouted as we pushed through the crowd.

Down the steps we went, deep into the heart of

the ship. "Remind me to pack my cocktail clothes the next time we decide to jump times," I asked Killian.

Even though I was running full tilt and was Killian running even faster, that vampire was gone. Killian put his arm out and slowed me down. The hallway stretching in front of us was completely empty with nothing but rows and rows of closed doors. She could have slipped into any one of the staterooms.

"You take that side, I'll take this one," I said, jiggling the handles. It was a wasted effort. They were all locked. Our lady and her boy toys gave us the slip. We lost her.

"Fuck," I said.

"Once again, you and I are of one mind," Killian said, giving the last door handle a frustrated jerk.

"Where did that crazy vampire go?" I asked. "You know we can't go back to our time until we find her."

Killian nodded grimly. "It appears we will be earning our vacation pay."

"If that bastard Julio cuts our fee in half, I'm stealing the bathrobes. All of them. On the entire boat." I jerked my thumb back up towards where we came from. "Let's make sure the kid is all right. Maybe let her know her imaginary friends aren't going to disappear on her."

But Jackie was gone by the time we showed up. I was hoping that her nanny hustled her off to bed and not that some Other Side monster had snatched her.

I looked at Killian. "We gotta make sure nothing ate her," I said.

Killian paced the floor. "Should we even try to return to our own time?" he finally asked.

That was the million dollar question, wasn't it. I wanted to escape. Boy oh boy, I wanted to just open up a portal and go back to our nice cozy little stateroom and enjoy some room service on our employer's dime. But instead, I found myself saying, "We gotta fix this. It is probably one of those 'entire fate of the world hangs upon this moment' moments. As much as I would rather be at home watching *This Old (Haunted) House*, I think we've got our own renovation project right smack dab in front of our nose." I looked off at the spot where Jackie had her meltdown. "Vampires are freaky, but I wonder what she saw that got her so scared?"

"I am not looking forward to finding out," said Killian.

"Hazard of the trade, my friend."

CHAPTER ELEVEN

"Hey! Jackie! You around here?" I called as we combed the boat floor-by-floor. We weren't having any sort of luck. "I sure hope she didn't fall into some random vortex," I muttered.

"It is a strange coincidence that the vampire we brought to Lacy had not been seen since 1936, and we find ourselves in that same time," Killian stated.

With everything going on, I had kind of forgotten about Lacy's phone call. Go figure it was still at the top of Killian's mind. More likely it was her top that was at the top of his mind.

"Yet in 1936, this boat should be in the middle of the ocean," he continued. "But we are docked in Long Beach."

"What are you getting at, Killian?"

I could tell his brain was working overtime on this thought. "Time does not seem to be trapped just within these walls, but into the world beyond us, too. California life seems to exist beyond the doors. This boat seems to exist independently from the true Empress Adelaide."

I mused. "It would have to be more than just an alternate timeline. Perhaps an alternate dimensional pocket...?" I shook my head. "It makes it awfully convenient, though, doesn't it?"

"What is convenient?"

"It is completely easy to keep tabs on vampires with today's registries, but to grab vampires from the past and bring them over? Who would notice a bunch of vampires disappearing from California eighty-odd years ago? They could pop on through this portal and walk into modern life and no one would even notice." I put my hand out and a modern ghost couple walked right through it. "The veil is so thin here. I bet natural portals open more regularly than the buffet in the grand ballroom."

"I wonder how many vampires have come through?" Killian thought aloud.

I really wish he hadn't. I started to do the math. I'm not what one would call a whiz, but the column of "possible number of vampires ferried over" in my ledger seemed a little scary. "So, Vaclav in our time keeps trying to tear down the boundary and bring over vampires. Think this is his new tactic?"

"It is an excellent informed hypothesis. If he had not upset the balance of ghosts upon this boat..."

"...if they are actually ghosts..."

"...and if there had not been management in place that cared about these otherworldly connections, he could have emptied The Other Side completely and we would not have even known."

"Maybe if Vaclav hadn't been so busy playing time-travel planner, Mr. Smith wouldn't have gotten a jump on him in Ghost Town and turned him into a werepire."

"Does the fact there still are vampires in the past indicate that you and I are successful now? Or is it unfolding in present day and the actions of the past have no impact upon history as it unfolds?"

"This makes my brain hurt."

"I believe the phrase you taught me was 'Do not sprain your brain,' correct?" said Killian dryly.

The elf had been hanging out with me too long.

We passed a sign that seemed like it could be a solution to some of our issues. Raiding a laundry room for clothes seemed awfully Marx Brothers, but if our life was going to turn into a movie, I'd prefer a screwball comedy than running around in our skivvies like some farce. Or teen slasher flick. "Come on, follow me."

The place was deserted, it being the middle of the night and all. Vats of hot water held used bed sheets and massive ringers lined a wall.

"What are you looking for, Maggie?" Killian asked.

"Clothes. Uniforms. Anything that can disguise us a bit," I said, looking through the stacks. "Here we go!" Over by the big ironing presses were a bunch of uniforms, freshly starched. "I knew these fancy first class accommodations wouldn't leave us high and dry."

I threw a porter's outfit at Killian as I grabbed some maid gear.

"This will be helpful?" he asked, looking skeptical.

I gave his pointy ears a good hard look and tossed him a hat. "Trust me. The help can go wherever they want and no one bats an eye."

Killian took off his shirt, revealing his chiseled

elfin perfection.

"Okay, maybe with you, they'll bat an eye," I said, unfolding my maid's uni.

He gave me a wink. "Are you batting an eye?"

"I'll bat your eye if you look over here while I'm changing." I stripped down and climbed into a nice little black number with a frilly collar and sleeves, starched apron, and paper hat. I slipped my utility belt under the skirt. It was a little lumpier than a petticoat, but I hoped the fashion police would give me a pass on account of the whole 'survival' thing.

"The maid look suits you."

"Save it for Lacy," I replied.

"Your neck guard and boots certainly add something," he said.

"I call this look clean and kickass."

"I would hire your services." Killian looked around. "Now, what shall we do with our former attire?"

"Eh, I guess we have to abandon it." I looked sadly at my pants. "So hard to find leather that fits right."

Killian walked over and grabbed my stack from me. "Maggie, if we are in the same space, but different time, we merely have to hide these where our future selves will find them."

"You'd think you'd been watching Bill and Ted!" I grinned. "Excellent, Killian!"

"I do not get that reference."

"It was an 80's movie... never mind. We have some serious cultural exchange issues we need to get through when we get finished up with our little project." I waved him to follow. "Let's go find a good hiding spot."

As we walked along, our clothes folded up like we were just returning some freshly laundered awesomeness to a guest, I felt the strangest thing. It was as we passed this big hallway. I felt this whoosh. It was like all the air had been sucked out of the room. A few more steps and the vacuum of energy was gone. I stopped Killian, who looked at me quizzically. I stepped backwards into the hallway intersection. There was the vacuum again. The fact I had been feeling absolutely nothing up until this point, and then got walloped by something big like that—it did not bode well.

"What is it, Maggie?"

"Just feeling like maybe we might have stumbled upon the key to what's going on."

Killian looked down the hallway, then back at me.

"What do you say we start servicing some rooms?" I asked.

CHAPTER TWELVE

Force of habit, I checked all the handles as we passed by. As expected, the doors were locked. I knew they didn't have what we were looking for, though. It was like getting swept along in a stream. Just follow the suck and we'd find out what was going on. Kind of like my life.

"Do you hear that?" I asked.

"Hear what?" asked Killian.

It was soft and distant, and could have been mistaken for a cat in heat. "Music. Organ music. Really bad organ music."

I wandered down the hallway some more. "Shoot, you'd think if you had an eternity to practice *The Maple Leaf Rag*, you'd be better."

The feeling was coming from the same spot where the music was, both of which were behind, surprise, a locked door. I knelt down, fumbled through my apron pockets, and pulled out my lock-pick set.

"Where did you acquire that?" asked Killian,

looking a little impressed.

"I was a Monster Scout. And you know that old motto..." I fumbled with the keyhole. Fortunately, it was simple technology and cooperating nicely for me. "Be prepared... so that you don't get your face eaten off."

The lock clicked and I pushed the door slowly open. In the middle of the room was a man tied to the organ. He was probably early fifties with thinning, red, sticky-outie hair. He was tall and gaunt and had a face like a mashed potato. He wore a burgundy suit and bolero tie, looking like he probably belonged in a saloon tinkling the keys while some gun fighters pulled aces out of their sleeves more than on an art deco cruise ship in the middle of the Long Beach harbor. But here he was. My first instinct was to run over and untie him, if just to get him to stop playing. My second instinct was to first figure out why he was tied to an organ and then figure out whether I should leave him tied up or ask him to join our party of merry mercenaries.

"Do you know *Piano Man*?" I asked as I edged forward.

He looked up from his keyboard and gasped, "Finally! An audience."

The guy was nuts, 100% certifiably bonkers. His eyes were crazy and he seemed to have forgotten that normal people blink. A big strip of metal bolted his waist to the back of his seat. Whoever did this left his arms and legs free so that he might share his music of the night, but that was about it.

"You might get more people if you let folks know you were chained up down here," I replied, pointing at his fancy harness. "But since you mentioned it, why are you chained up down here?"

"Ah, I did not mention it, you did," he said, waving his finger knowingly as if I was trying to pull a fast one on him.

"You caught me! So why don't you say why."

He played an ominous chord. "I play the song for the lady in black..."

I thought back to our nice little cruise director up there poolside. "I think I know her."

"You know Barbara?" he said, suddenly friendly in that way you get when you figure out you have something in common with a complete stranger.

"Know 'of' Barbara," I replied. "Remind me what she does, again?"

He faded a bit and then started playing again. "She ferries the undead from this world to the world beyond, but every night, she joins me, she tells me to make my music until the world stops."

I couldn't get a pulse on what made this guy tick and whether he fell into the 'good crazy organ player' or 'evil crazy organ player' category. "So... do you like making music until the world stops?"

"Oh yes!"

"And you like this lady in black?"

He started playing some very sad chords. "No, but she is the only one who visits me."

"We're visiting you."

He perked right up at that. "Indeed! You are!"

"If we were to free you, would you try to say... eat us?"

"Oh no!" he replied with great horror in his eyes. "I'm vegan."

"Good! This is good!" I turned to Killian. We stood there looking at each other in silence for a bit before I said, "So... I think we should let him go."

"Maggie?" Killian replied, stopping me in that way that seemed like maybe he was doubting my decision making skills. "Do you think that is sound?"

"Listen, the vampires want him playing this organ. Which makes me want to make sure he's not playing this organ."

"But I like to play the organ!" the guy protested.

"Sorry, I didn't get your name..." I said.

"Mortimer."

"Mortimer, you can play all the organs you like, just not this organ."

He stroked the keys lovingly. "But why not this organ?"

"I think it might cause the world to end."

"Is that so terrible?"

"You won't be able to play the organ after the world ends," I pointed out.

He took a moment and then agreed, "True."

"So, if you want to play the organ for eternity, and who doesn't, we gotta get you out of there." I turned to Killian and handed him my gun. "Killian? I'm about to do something really stupid. If necessary, I'm going to need you to shoot us."

He slowly took the gun out of my hands. "On most days, dear Maggie, I would be overjoyed at the prospect. But why might you want me to shoot you now?"

"Because I'm about to see if Mortimer is telling us the truth."

I walked over and held out my hand to the guy. "If we free you, do I have your word that you will not kill or harm either myself or my partner?"

He looked at my proffered hand, then back up

at me.

"I do not touch other hands," he apologized. "It is unhygienic."

Great, I had a crazy, OCD, bad musician of doom.

"How would you suggest that we agree to work together on this little mission, then?"

Mortimer looked at my hand and then looked at me again. He clenched his teeth and held out his hand. I grasped it quickly. It was cold, but not dead cold. I'm pretty sure he had a pulse in his body, which ruled out the undead, which ruled out a ton of bad monsters. No zings of power. And he didn't try to bite me, which was an even better sign. Plus, if he was germaphobic, it was good to know I could bypass the staking when a sneeze would do just as well.

"Deal." I turned to Killian. "All right, partner. Let's get him out of here."

CHAPTER THIRTEEN

It took quite a bit of doing, but we finally unshackled Mortimer thanks to my lock pick set and Killian's ability to talk me down when I was ready to find a fire ax and chop the thing to bits.

As soon as Mortimer was out and stretching, I took the opportunity to examine this thing he was chained to so as to figure out how it worked.

"What's so special about this organ?" I asked him.

"I am the only one who can play it," he replied.

"And some days, not even that," I muttered under my breath as I poked at one of the keys. No sound came out. "So how comes it doesn't work for me?"

"It knows my blood."

Killian and I exchanged glances. I crouched down to get a good look at the under-carriage. There it was. You had your normal foot pedals down there, but on either side, there were two spikes that looked like they were covered in some old, rust-colored something.

"Shit."

Killian got down to look with me. "Is that what I think it is?"

"Yep."

We had run into this kind of magic before. There was a door in Vaclav's castle that barred fairies and vampires from opening it. The spike needed human blood to open. Looked like Vaclav had done some research and development and figured out how to upgrade his door design to make an organ that ran on blood magic, too.

I looked at Mortimer. "Are you human?"

He shook his head, "No. Siren."

I gave him the old fisheye. "Sirens are girls."

He shrugged, "And therein is the eternal tragedy of my life. My sisters sit upon the cliffs, calling the sailors to dash themselves upon the shore. But as a male, my vocal cords do not possess the power of the hunter. My voice will lure no food stuff to throw itself upon our rocks for harvest. But I have been told my organ playing is magical. And so, I play for the enjoyment and amusement of all, since my prowess is ill-fitted for any other use."

"While I'm sure it sucks to be you, I'm actually kind of glad you are what you are," I replied. "So we have ourselves a magical organ and a magical creature playing it." There was a tube attached to the wall. I pointed at it. "What does that do, Mortimer?"

He looked at it. "The pipe is connected to the smokestack. When I play the right notes, it takes the music and opens the doors."

"What do you mean it opens the doors?"

"Three times tonight, upon the hour, I was to give a command performance, and the notes would play simultaneously across three times and three dimensions to open the doors so that they can come through."

I looked at Killian. "Harmonics to open portals?"

He shrugged, "You tell me, Maggie."

"Vaclav is using harmonics to open portals," I told him. "There was the portal in the swimming pool, but that was naturally occurring. I mean, someone obviously gave folks a hand to open it, but the veil was willing."

"But, if we were to hazard a guess, this more likely has to do with that large portal you observed in the bulkhead, does it not?"

Killian and I locked eyes.

"Shit."

I picked up our stacks of clothes, remembering one of the reasons why Killian and I had been skulking around in the first place. "If we survive all this, remember that we hid our stuff behind the homicidal musical instrument that may or may not cause the collapse of the dimensional wall."

"I shall make note," remarked Killian dryly.

I turned to Mortimer. "Hey! Mortimer, we need to go find out how much trouble we're all in. You wanna come? Stay? What're you feeling like?"

He rubbed his wrists and looked longingly at the organ.

I reached out and grabbed his hand, steering him towards the doors so that Killian could take over babysitting duties. "Sorry, that just turned rhetorical. You're coming with us."

I did one last idiot-check around the room to make sure we hadn't forgotten any lifesaving magical artifacts, and then smoothed out my apron and straightened my cap. "Alrighty. Let's get this party swinging."

Killian and I took off for the stairs with Mortimer in tow and started racing down the hall. I suddenly stopped and slapped my forehead. "Jackie. We need to find Jackie."

This time Killian grabbed me and pushed me in front of him: "After we save the world."

"What if she is the key to saving the world?"

"If what we think is down in that hull is down in that hull, the safest place for that child will be 'not with us,' I believe."

"You have a point."

We reached the stairway and just headed down. Down, down, down until there was no more down to go. The sounds of the engines thrummed. We crept out onto the shadowy catwalk where we could get a good look at the bottom of the boat without anyone seeing us.

The hole was glowing white hot with fire. I had never seen a portal that huge in my entire frickin' life. And there were vampires pouring through. One after another, they were filling up the ship, marching in lock step one after another.

Killian, Mortimer, and I crouched down and got really still, like prairie dogs spotting a hawk. Fortunately, there was enough chaos that no one was looking our way. But it wasn't much comfort knowing 'there was enough chaos going on' to keep a vampire from looking our way. There was a guy who seemed to be in charge. He had a clipboard, so I was just guessing. He was marking off passengers as they came through. All of the vampires were dressed like modern day folks, which raised a couple concerns in my brain, along the lines that these travelers weren't too concerned with blending into this particular decade.

"Fuck," I whispered.

"Can you close the portal?" asked Killian.

I shook my head, "I'm good, but I'm not that good. That thing is huge."

I crept back and motioned for the fellas to follow me. There was nothing we could do here besides turn ourselves into a snack from some hungry passengers, so we retreated up the stairs to regroup and strategize.

"Okay, what do we know?" I asked.

"The one smokestack became illuminated and we were transported to this other time," said Killian. "It also opened this portal door, allowing the vampire army to come through."

"And how many smokestacks does this boat have?"

"Three."

I pointed at Mortimer. "We have the one guy who can play the organ that can open up these portals."

"This is a positive on our side."

I started getting a little excited. "So that means they must have to take several jumps."

"Inform me how this is good news...?"

I looked at him. I swear that elf never listened. "Dimensions are like pieces of paper. They stack one on top of the other. If you are at the bottom of the stack and want to get to the top, you have to punch through all of the dimensions in between. So they need to do three jumps before they can invade."

"And so...?"

"So, we have two opportunities to stop them from reaching present time, which means, that while there might be hundreds of them, it takes a whole lot longer for them to jump, and with the three of us, we can jump higher and faster. We might be small, but we are mighty! Let's get to that swimming pool."

CHAPTER FOURTEEN

Killian guided us through the maze of hallways, all of us slowing down as if everything was perfectly normal whenever we passed passengers or someone who looked like maybe they could haul us off for a good scolding for our unprofessionalism. But the moment we were out of their sight, bam, off we ran.

I knew we had made it to the swimming pool by the sound of splashing. No one was borrowing towels from their room and wandering down in their flip flops.

Killian, Mortimer, and I stopped. Killian and I flanked either side of the door while Mortimer stood there like some country bumpkin on his first trip to the big, bright city.

"Try to pretend you belong here," I hissed at him.

He managed to close his mouth so that his jaw wasn't hanging open, but he was still looking around in wonder like Oliver Twist in a sweet shop.

I whispered at Killian, "Okay, we're not doing big

heroics or anything like that. We barge through these doors and head straight for the vortex."

Mortimer looked disappointed. "No dip in the pool?"

"I promise to get you a membership to the YMCA as soon as it looks like we aren't going to die," I hissed.

Killian and I locked eyes and on the count of three, we pushed the doors open and ran inside.

Guys and dolls, or whatever they referred to fancy ladies and gents in the 1930's, were splashing about in the water. Most were hanging to the edges and yakking up a storm, but a couple were doing laps and taking advantage of the diving board.

I looked over and there was Jackie playing with her family. Poor kid, it looked like something she might have done before. As in, done in an eternal loop before. I wondered how long these people had been stuck on this boat, thinking that one day they were eventually going to arrive at their destination. From the look on Jackie's face, it had been awhile.

I scoped out the place to see if the coast was clear, and, as our luck would have it, that was when the doors opened on The Other Side of the room revealing our favorite vampire tour guide and a group of four people who looked like they were in serious need of a spray tan.

Jackie screamed as the woman in black came through, then shouted at everyone around her, "Run away! It is not safe! Run away!"

Everyone in the pool seemed to have been through this part of the drill enough to know what was coming next and how they did not want to be a part of it. They scattered like someone had shouted

"Fire!" in a movie theatre.

All except for our party.

"Yoohoo! Barbara!" Mortimer called out to her, waving as if he was so excited to see an old friend. "I am not going to be playing organ any more for you! I hope we can work together in the future, though! I appreciate the opportunity!"

"Son of a bitch," I said as I tried to push him behind a column before our lady in black realized someone was not locked up where he was supposed to be. But Barbara was smarter than she looked. And, may I state for the record, she was looking like an idiot, fangs out and hissing in public. Vampires these days. There is no shame. No skulking around corners. Just full on attack-mode, even if there are children present. No wonder The Other Side kept them under such tight wraps.

I took off my maid hat and handed it to Killian. "Hold this. I'm going in."

Killian handed it to Mortimer as he took off after me. "Right behind you, partner."

I pulled my stakes out of my sleeves. Killian pulled out his pole from God only knows where. Someday I was going to have to ask him about that. Preferably, I'd have an opportunity after we finished killing these stowaways.

We were on the vampires in a second. The humans in the pool were still screaming and scattering, taking their time to get out as they put on their socks and shoes and blouses and pants and skirts and whatever else they felt they needed to do to maintain their modesty as death breathed down their necks. I felt the boat shake when I staked the first vampire. This little time/space bubble didn't seem to like when someone came along and messed with its rhythm. I was more than happy to drop this beat.

Barbara was pissed, though. She looked over at where Mortimer was standing. Here, as we were fighting for life and death, he was apologetically explaining that he couldn't play the rest of the night, but he hoped to work again with her in the future and hoped this decision wouldn't reflect poorly upon his professionalism and dedication to the organ. Musicians. Always looking for the next gig. I could tell Barbara was looking for several organs she could remove him from.

"Mortimer! Get behind that column!" I shouted as a vampire came at me. His fangs banged right up against my neck guard. I made sure to twist my stake as I pushed it through his chest, the fucker.

Barbara seemed like she was really torn with whether to go after Mortimer or hop through the portal. So, she did what any desperate villain will do. She took a hostage. She grabbed our Jackie and jumped. She made sure to leave us with some company so that we weren't lonely, though.

By this time, all of the human types had fled the pool. The room was shaking in and out of reality, giving everything a fuzzy edge. This bubble was getting pretty darn unstable, which I was thrilled to pieces about. Nothing like a collapsing dimension to put a little hustle in your bustle.

Only two more vampires remained. The one came flashing at me with his fangs gleaming like the mother-of-pearl ceiling overhead. He might not bleed when he flossed, but he bled just fine when I stuck him through the heart. I leaned over and rested my hands on my knees, breathing deep.

I was tuckered.

"Maggie, behind you!" Killian shouted.

Someone forgot to tell this new vamp that the #1 rule of the swimming pool is no running on the deck. I didn't even look. I just raised my arm and let the vampire stake himself as he rushed me. I yanked it out and let him fall to the ground.

"She took Jackie!" I shouted at Killian.

"I know!" Killian replied, moving towards the portal like maybe we should make our way through.

"I told you that kid was going to end up being the lynchpin to the world's survival!"

"You did. You were right. I was wrong. Are you happy enough that we can go save her now?" asked Killian.

"Say that you were wrong once more."

"I was wrong."

I stood up. "Cool. Let's go."

I jogged over to Mortimer and grabbed his arm. He clung to the column.

"It's okay to come out now," I said.

He instantly relaxed. "Well, why didn't you say so? I was just following orders. Hide, Mortimer. Run away, Mortimer. Stop playing organ so the world does not end, Mortimer. It is hard to keep all the rules straight all at once."

I clapped him on the shoulders. "Don't you worry that pretty little ginger head of yours, I'll do all the thinking for us." I motioned to the portal. "Right now, we are going to go jump through there, try to save a little girl, and hopefully stop the end of the world. Ready?"

He straightened his jacket and fixed his tie. He pulled down his shirt cuffs and smoothed his hair.

He gave me a nod and then informed me, "I am ready now."

"Fantastic." I looked at Killian. "How about you, partner?"

He nodded, "After you."

I leapt through the portal.

And landed in the middle of the same room. I mean, same room, different time. The vampire corpses had disappeared and the pool was filled with a bunch of shirtless menfolk with neat haircuts.

They looked at me like I had grown horns. Guess they don't see too many women in the middle of the ocean, whatever bizarre in-between-worlds ocean we were floating in.

"Hey boys!" I said, giving them a little finger wave and edged towards the exit. "Just stopped by to see if you needed any fresh towels. How's the water? Peachy, I'm sure. Anyone seen a woman dressed in black with a little girl in tow?"

And at that moment Barbara decided to show her ugly face. She flew at me out of the men's dressing room.

"Hey! Since when did this become a co-ed joint?!" I shouted as I got my foot between me and her chest and kicked her back. One of the gents, dressed in a 1940s dough boy uniform, had a hold of Jackie and was dragging her out of the room.

"Where is Mortimer?!" Barbara hissed as she came at me all claws and nails. She was strong. Wicked strong. And the men around me seemed pretty content to sit back and watch the catfight.

"Aren't any of you going to help me?" I asked them as I struggled to get Barbara off me again.

Now, I know that there are plenty of men who pay

good money to see two chicks battle it out, but these guys suddenly bared their teeth and looked very upset about the fact I suggested breaking this party up.

And that's when I realized I was in a swimming pool of the undead.

"What the hell is going on here?" I asked.

"Just some of Uncle Sam's boys returning home from Europe," Barbara announced as she tried to slam my head against the pool tiles.

"This would go a whole lot easier if we could sit down and discuss this like rational adults." I rolled away, picked up a heavy deck chair, and tossed it in her general direction. She danced easily out of its path as it flew by, but I took the opportunity of that momentary distraction to get back on my feet.

Barbara ran out of the room. The vampires around us just leaned back and went back to a state of droneness.

"Why aren't you attacking?" I asked as I walked close to one of them. He didn't even flinch when I staked him.

That's when Killian and Mortimer decided to finally show up.

"Sorry," Killian apologized. "Mortimer was worried about traveling without his toothbrush."

Mortimer gave a shrug. "Your body only produces one set of adult teeth. If you do not take care of them, you will lose them."

I rolled my eyes. "I should have left him shackled to that organ."

"What did we miss?" asked Killian.

I waved at the room. "Well, we landed in a pool filled with vampires, but they don't seem hungry."

Killian crouched down and looked at them. He

even reached over and opened up one of the guy's eyes, which is far braver than I'll ever be. He shook his head. "They must be dying. Or starving. Or in a state of suspension."

"You are not helping at all," I mentioned.

Killian wiped his hand on his porter's jacket and pointed at all the uniforms folded up and stacked around the edges of the room. "My guess is that they are soldiers from this time that have been turned, for whatever reason. They look to be in day one or two of the three-day transformation. Perhaps men who were in the wrong place at the wrong time and saw too much."

"Sucks to be them," I said.

"So to speak."

I looked at them. "Well, do we stake them now or wait for them to turn mean and stake them later?"

"If they live to see The Other Side of transformation, there is the possibility of future employment opportunities if we wait for later..."

"Are you saying why stake for free when you could be paid?"

"There is that whole 'survival' aspect of it to consider..."

"Overrated." I rubbed my shoulder. I was feeling beat to hell from all of this and didn't feel the need to go for any Exceeds Expectations gold stars. "Okay," I pointed at the door, "she got away, which doesn't make me feel too good about life right now. Usually when people run away, they're running to something, and I'm betting her destination involves dangerous things that could be used to make our lives miserable. Or short. Or miserable AND short."

"That would not be ideal," replied Killian.

I took Mortimer's hand and drug him across the pool as far away from the vortex in the dressing room that I could manage. "We need to get Jackie, keep Mortimer safe, and destroy that organ."

"Sounds like a typical day at K&M Tracking."

"That's M&K Tracking," I corrected.

"We shall discuss."

"How about whoever stakes the woman in black gets to decide?"

Killian put out his hand. "You have yourself a wager."

CHAPTER FIFTEEN

I pointed down the hallway. The boat in this day and age had been transformed from its state of lovely art deco grandeur to a military wet dream. The carpet had been ripped up in favor of battleship linoleum. The walls covered in sheets of plywood painted military grey. All semblance of artsy-fartsy-ness replaced with industrial efficiency.

The thing I noticed most, though, was that this floor was eerily quiet. I'd place cash money on the fact our lady in black and her cohorts wanted to make sure no one figured out they had some VIPs lounging by the pool. It was brilliant, really. Who was to notice if a bunch of soldiers disappeared en route rather than on the battlefield? The only one who would care would be their commander and dollars to donuts, their commander had developed an allergy to Vitamin D somewhere along the way.

But Killian and I didn't have time to worry about the bloodsuckers here. Hopefully, if we played our cards right, they'd all disappear into the netherworld in a paradoxical time conundrum. Actually, hopefully this whole entire alternate universe boat would blink out and the only thing that would remain were the normal, grumpy ghosts in the normal, grumpy timeline of modern day. Mom would be so proud, me sweeping away the riff raff to make space for some of her favorite buddies.

"You doing okay, Mortimer?" I asked over my shoulder as we jogged.

"My! Look at how things have changed!" he replied, all wide-eyed and a little bewildered by it all. "I think that I like the world as it was before."

"You and me both." I turned to Killian. "Thoughts on where you would hide a small child on a boat full of strapping undead men?"

"The one spot where she needs us to go?" Killian replied.

"The organ room," we both said in unison.

"Do we just go barging in there with guns blazing?"

Killian shrugged. "Strange as it might be to believe, I have not been in this situation before."

"Well, what good are you?" I asked.

"Dock my pay."

"I am so charging Julio mileage for all this time-travel," I commented.

"What is the per diem for seventy years?"

"I'm thinking $.39 a minute, which I think equals out to a billion dollars."

"I shall prepare the invoice," Killian replied.

I heard a little girl's screams from down the corridor.

"Come on. This way," I said.

Thanks to Jackie, we were all on high alert when we turned the corner, which is the only reason that we weren't creamed by the vampires when they ambushed us. Still, they cut our work out for us. Barbara was on the far end, but I lost sight of her behind the hulking crew. There were twelve of them in a cramped hallway, all of them ex-military. The only thing we had going for us is that they weren't armed with guns. The bullets would have ricocheted inside the bulkhead like ping-pong balls inside a lottery bubble. But that meant they had big sharp knives and big pointy teeth instead. Got me thinking that as soon as we wiped the floor with them, I might get back into something a little sturdier than a maid's uniform.

I saw Jackie curled in a doorjamb just before a knife came flying at me. I ducked to the side with about a hair's breadth of space between me and permanent shishkabob-ness. I winged my silver stake and got the guy right in the heart. The good news about the 1940's was that the only folks wearing Kevlar were me and Killian. The bad news was that we were outnumbered six-to-one and my stake was now ten feet across the room impaled in the chest of a bad guy.

I turned around and started yanking the knife he threw at me out of the wall. I mean, if he wasn't going to use it, finders keepers and all that. It was pretty well embedded and I had two vampires on me before I could yank it out. I elbowed one of them in the teeth and caught the other one in the stomach with the tip of my steel-toed boot. I know they weren't quite regulation to the uniform, but I'd take the reprimand. I looked like a maid and I was cleaning up. I don't see how anyone could complain.

Killian had two of the vampires staked on either side of his pole and was lifting them up like a strongman doing a clean-and-jerk at the same time he kicked a vampire coming at him, square in the chest.

"I didn't know your pole had pointy ends!" I shouted appreciatively.

"I am a mystery wrapped up in an enigma, Maggie!" he yelled back as he flung the two vampires off and lined up to skewer another one.

I got the knife out of the wall and did a little impromptu open heart surgery on my attackers.

Jackie watched in horror as I dispatched the last of my monsters. When I was done, I leaned up against the wall and slid to the floor next to her, breathing hard. The vampires managed to tear my pretty dress and scrape up my knuckles, but other than that, I was in fairly good shape. I patted her knee and tried to be comforting. "It's okay, kid. The monsters are all gone."

I wasn't about to tell her about all of the other ones on this boat.

Killian rolled over and staked the last vampire he was grappling with on the ground.

"You alive?" I asked.

He nodded painfully. "Did we win?"

"We won." I looked around the room. It was just us three. Fuck. "But we lost Mortimer."

Killian wiped the sweat from his brow on his arm. "Did you stake our lady in black?"

"Not yet, but I'm not losing our bet, elf."

"I really think that you'll find K&M Tracking has such a lovely ring to it," Killian said, reaching out his hand to me. "Let us return Jackie to her own time and find our organist. Are you coming?"

"Guess enough sitting around for the day." I looked over at Jackie. "Want to go home?"

Jackie nodded. "Will she come back?"

"We'll get her," I promised. I reached out my hand and took her grubby little paw in mine. "Sorry you had to see all that."

"It is okay. Sometimes that happens."

She just saw a maid and a porter off twelve vampires. I liked this kid's style. "Sure does, Jackie."

We slowly got up and walked out into the hallway towards the pool area. Or at least where I hoped the pool area was. Looked like my tracker skills were working just about as well as they were in that past dimension.

"So, Jackie. Is that short for anything?" I asked, trying to make conversation.

She nodded proudly. "Jocelyn. Jocelyn Dolan Duffy."

I stopped dead in the middle of the hallway. "Say that again."

"Jocelyn Dolan Duffy," she said.

Killian looked at me. "What is it, Maggie?"

"I think it might be really important that we keep her safe," I replied.

"Why?"

I pointed at the kid. "Killian, I would like to introduce you to my grandmother."

CHAPTER SIXTEEN

"What?" Killian asked, his concentration absolutely broken.

I pointed at Jackie. "Yeah, I am pretty sure this kid grows up to my grandmom."

"Are you positive?" Killian asked.

"Kinda escalates our present situation to a major conundrum if my biological grandmother is trapped in a time bubble that the vampires control, doesn't it?"

"It is an excellent strategy for ensuring you are not born," he pointed out, admiringly.

"I should have thought of this myself. I'd go back far enough to stake Vaclav when he is still wearing his training teeth."

Killian bent down to Jackie. "Tell me where you are from?"

"London!" she said. "But we were from Ireland before that. We had to go to England in order to come to America."

Killian looked at me for confirmation.

"We got our ancestor."

She laughed, "I'm not old enough to be a grandmother."

"Yeah, well... you will be someday. Hopefully." I turned to Killian, "I'm pretty sure I've broken all sorts of time-travel, dimensional laws."

"I believe the vampires started it."

"Okay, the facts are these. We are in charge of my own grandmother. We need to get Jackie into the past, but out of a bubble that the vampires control. At the same time, we need to find Mortimer and make sure he doesn't play that organ." I looked at my watch. "And seeing how that first bell went off at 10:00, I'm thinking the next should be at 11:00. Looks like we have about forty-five minutes to do all this."

Killian rubbed his face. "Let us first secure her safety. Then, save the world?"

"I say we save the world, then secure her safety."

"There will not be a world if we do not save her, first."

"If we save her first, there might not be a world around left to save."

"I can take care of myself!" she shouted.

"She is most definitely your grandmother," Killian replied.

"It's genetic."

"I can see."

"Okay, how about this. We jump backwards and stick her where she needs to go and hopefully, when we pop this bubble, she'll be exactly where she needs to be to go back to where she belongs."

"Does time and space work like that?"

"I have no idea."

He held up his hand and said, "Let us proceed, Maggie. It is your future... or past... you understand what I mean."

We got to the swimming pool with its vampire soup. No sign of either Mortimer or Barbara, just a bunch of guys who looked like they really would have rather been dead. I grabbed Jackie's hand as if my life depended upon it, because it did, and got ready to jump through the portal.

Things were getting a little bleedy with space, though. The room was overlapping with the future and I could see a woman in a flowered shirt from a generic bargain store in the swimming area. She pointed at us, her eyes grow wide. I looked at Killian and jerked my thumb back, "She can see us."

He peered at her. Her husband and a group of other folks appeared, too. They were transparent and you could see the entire boat straight through them. Guess we managed to hit the perfect timing to run into the modern day candlelight ghost tour. They were all fumbling around with their cell phones. It was almost as if this time and that time were layered upon one another like two pieces of celluloid. I wasn't taking a hankering to this movie, though, and kind of wanted my money back.

"Why are there ghosts here?" Jackie asked. "There are always so many ghosts on this boat!"

"They aren't ghosts," I replied. "You're looking into the future."

"Why are all the people in the future in their underwear?" she whispered.

I looked around at all the tourists in their tank tops and shorts. Yeah, it kind of did look like maybe they forgot to put on some clothes.

I didn't want to freak her out that in a couple decades these people would be looking positively prudish, thank you 1980's, so I just said, "Oh... just... fashion."

She wrinkled her nose, "I think I would like to stay in my own time."

"You and me both."

The woman was freaking out even more, pointing and shouting. I grabbed Killian's hand and yanked him and Jackie around the corner where the group couldn't stare at us.

"Fuck," I said.

Jackie looked up at me. "You swear like a saaaailor," she said through squinty eyes.

"Out of the mouths of babes, Maggie?" Killian asked.

"Shut up, elf. We're on a boat, aren't we?" I pointed out. I peered around the corner, getting a glimpse of the tourists. They were freaking out like they just won the grand prize on a game show. "Well, the good news is that Julio got the haunting he was looking for and we can probably claim our full paycheck for that little stunt."

"That is good news!" said Killian. "What is the bad news?"

"I think that portal goes in only one direction."

"What?"

"I think if we go through, we'll be bringing my grandma into the future. Then, we'll have a fantastic two jumps to navigate before we can get her into the past."

"Two..." Killian said.

I chewed on the inside of my lip. "We can't go

through," I said finally. "We can't risk it."

"Good!" said Jackie. "I can help you!"

"You'll be the most helpful if you just say alive, kid."

"So, what do we do with your grandmother while we save the world?" asked Killian.

"I can help!" Jackie repeated like we hadn't heard her the first time.

"Engine room!" I exclaimed.

"Engine room?"

"Yep. I'm thinking we might have ourselves what you might call the best babysitter in as many dimensions as you can shake a stick at."

Killian looked like he wasn't convinced. I held a finger to my lips and pointed around. Didn't want to blow my plan in case any of those vampires were listening. And more important, I didn't want Killian to try and convince me otherwise if it was super stupid.

The ghosts of ghost-tours-yet-to-come were fighting their way over to where we were hidden, so I motioned to Killian and the kid that we needed to hightail it out of there.

"Hey, Killian?" I asked as we jogged out.

"Yes, Maggie?"

"Do you remember at all how to actually get to the engine room?"

"Are you asking if an elf remember his way to a place he has been before?" Killian smiled. "What would you do without me, tracker? Come along. This way!"

We followed him down the steps, trying to look like we belonged as we passed a bunch of GIs. I'm not sure how convincing we were. In fact, I'm pretty sure we weren't convincing at all. But we were able to buy some time as they figured out whether to report us to their commanding officer or not, and we made it to the engine room safe and sound.

I started calling, "George! George the Gargoyle! Where are you?!"

I heard a scrabbling sound as he crawled out of God only knows what hole.

The gargoyle jumped up on the railing, wiping his fingers on an oily rag in his hip pocket. "Funny seeing you here." He looked at our outfits. "Having a nice weekend?"

I looked at him. "Wait. How do you know us? We don't meet for another seventy years."

"Let's just say we've met before."

"Right... Are you jumping through time with us or are you being literal?"

George shrugged. "What is time? A false construct of human existence to mark the passing of perception."

"That's pretty deep."

"We gargoyles have plenty of time to think."

Jackie was starting to wander off, completely bored. We needed to get this show on the road. "Listen, George, any chance you are up for a holy mission?"

He got really quiet and said, "Now, you wouldn't be offering me stuff like that if you didn't mean it, did you?"

"I'm not one to take the Lord's name in vain."

Killian elbowed me in the ribs. "Yes, you are."

"Jesus, Killian, quit blowing my cover. I'm trying to convince this gargoyle we need his help."

Killian shut up, but the gargoyle rolled his eyes.

"What is it?"

I grabbed Jackie's wrist and hauled her back over to us. I gave her a little twirl so George could get a good look at her.

He started laughing and got really close. Now, if I had been that kid, I would have been screaming and running for cover at this moment. Gargoyles are freaking scary. It's how they are able to scare off evil. But gotta hand it to her, Jackie just sat there and looked at him with curiosity. Guess this affinity for monsters really did run in the family.

"I recognize you," Jackie said. She pointed at the gargoyle. "I saw him before but he was a ghost!"

George gave a sort of 'aw shucks' swish of his head. "I wasn't a ghost..."

"Think of him more like a guardian angel," I said. "A slightly terrifying guardian angel. A gargoylian angel."

Jackie nodded, totally down with all of this.

"So, is this kid the holy mission you have for me, Maggie?" he asked.

"Pretty much. Turns out that a lot hangs in the balance of her survival and we need someone to hang out with her."

George pointed at all the gears in the engine room. "I got a job, Maggie."

"Nothing more important than this," I said.

He sighed, "Fine. I'll watch the kid."

"Good. Because a whole bunch of vampires might be after her. Make sure she doesn't bite it. Or that the vampires don't bite her."

George's eyes lit up. "Did you say vampires?"

"I did. Vampires."

He rubbed his hands together greedily. "Why

didn't you say so? I would have been on-board without a second thought!"

"Well, next time I'll make sure to mention it at the top of our negotiations."

But George was already moving on. He handed Jackie a wrench and was explaining to her, "Okay, kid. When you see the whites of their fangs, you just swing this and knock their block off."

Killian gave me a little pat, reminding me we had places to be, things to kill.

"Okay, Killian, let's go find Mortimer."

Jackie bounced the wrench up and down, looking entirely too excited about hitting things. Grandparents these days. They grow up so fast.

CHAPTER SEVENTEEN

The soldiers packed the hallways, going to and fro to the ballroom, which was now relegated to a mess hall. It wasn't quite the fancy buffet of Sunday brunch, but it had a certain symmetry to it all. I didn't look anything like a WAC, but I think they were just thrilled to pieces to have a nice set of stems to look at. I made sure to keep my skirt hitched high so there weren't any complaints. It also helped in case there was any running needed. Count the invention of spandex on my list of "awesome things in the future that I was missing a lot."

I looked down at my watch. Between the battle and that little side trip, we had about a half hour before the Ghost Spirit got sunk by the U-boat of time.

"Okay, Killian, so if you were an evil vampire trying to tear down the boundaries, where would you hide Mortimer?"

"Organ room?"

"Organ room."

"I would be willing to bet my life upon it."

"Lucky for you, you might just have the opportunity to place that bet."

"It seems like an opportunity that arises frequently when I am in your company, Maggie."

"Make your complaint to management," I replied as I peered around a corner. There was no one in sight and I waved to Killian that the coast was clear.

"If you are your own boss, is it your own fault for getting into terrible situations?" Killian asked.

"I feel like we live in an equal opportunity blame game."

"Then I blame you, Maggie."

"And I blame you. Now, shall we kick some vampire ass?"

"Gladly. Do you see one?"

I looked around the next corner. There were two soldiers standing guard. "Is that the organ room?" I asked Killian.

He snuck a look and nodded his head.

"I think we found ourselves our strategic target."

Killian crouched down beneath me so we could both look at them. The vampires hadn't smelled us yet, which made me believe these strapping young fellas were a little light on the brain rations. Young vampires are dumb as a box of hardtack. That said, they had a terrible habit of binge-eating.

"Surprise attack?" I suggested, palming my silver stake.

"Surprise attack it is," Killian replied, pulling out his staff.

We both started running. I really needed to get myself some of those fancy shoes that Killian wore.

They were so quiet, it's like he was running through a field of pillows, meanwhile my clunky shoes alerted every vampire and its mother we were on the way.

The good news is that all the noise made them turn square to us, which gave me the target I needed. I threw my stake and caught him. Unfortunately, my aim was a little off, so it was just poking out of his shoulder. He and his buddy turned tail and ran.

"Mortimer or the bad guys?" Killian asked.

"Bad guys. We're not much good if they sound the alarm and we have a whole army of vampires getting in our way."

"Good call," said Killian, doubling his speed.

"Besides, I want my stake back."

"Your sister would never forgive you if you lost it," Killian replied.

We saw the vampires duck into a stateroom. It happened to be the same stateroom that tour guide told us what seemed like a million years ago was the most haunted stateroom on the entire boat.

"Shit, Killian. You realize what room that is?"

He looked at it and said, "The good news is that perhaps the only poltergeists here are ourselves."

It actually was strangely comforting. I was feeling pretty good about busting up some furniture on this damned boat, and if it made our employer, in whatever dimension he was inhabiting right now, feel better about paying Killian and I, I would be more than happy to bust up everything in sight. Killian and I burst right through.

The stateroom in this place and time was as fancy as a captain's quarters with a decidedly feminine touch, which was completely out of step with the rest of the boat's decor. My guess was this was where

Barbara was entertaining the troops in her down-time, mainly because the room was filled with soldiers and they were looking under-entertained.

They hissed at Killian and me as we burst into the room.

"Trap?" I asked as I started to back slowly towards the door.

"Most decidedly," said Killian as the door was helpfully slammed shut by the vampire who had been behind it, waiting for us.

"Shit."

They were on us like a pack of lions on an injured zebra. The good news is that we, unlike the unfortunate zebra of the Sahara, happened to be armed. Still, close quarters made for some awkwardness and far too many public displays of destruction for my taste. I saw my stake in the shoulder of that one vampire, then I saw him rip it out and chuck it at me. I leaned to the side and it hit a vampire who had just been about to knock me on my ass.

"Thanks!" I shouted at the guy. Taking out his buddy didn't seem like what he had been hoping for.

They say that gratitude is an action, though, so I made sure to kill that vampire quick. I picked up my stake, wiped it on my skirt, and winged it at another guy right before I knifed another. I heard a swoosh and turned to see Killian slice a vamp's head clean off with the pointy end of his stick. It went flying and hit one of the vampire's friends, who looked for a moment like he wasn't sure whether to be upset about it or eat it. I saved him from being too torn between decisions by poking him through the heart. There was a howl of rage. I spun and caught the soldier trying to creep up on me. The howl probably wasn't the best strategy when trying to be sneaky. I was grateful he was sleeping in his crypt during that part of basic training.

Suddenly, I realized the room was really quiet. Too quiet. Not a gasp. Not a breath. I turned to look and saw I was all alone. Killian was gone.

Fuck.

Double fuck.

CHAPTER EIGHTEEN

I ran out into the hallway and looked right and left. God bless Killian, he wasn't going down without a fight. He had left huge gouge marks in the wall. I mean, sure they stopped abruptly, which was more than a little troubling, but he at least gave me a pointer as to which direction to run. And, man, I needed that direction. I felt as lost as a blonde in Boston. This boat had me so turned around, I couldn't have told you which way was up. This is not a good place to be when you have to figure out which way to take the staircase.

I decided that vampires probably would want to stick to someplace away from windows, preferably someplace where they wouldn't risk catching the beauty of a sunrise. Away from windows probably meant the cabin rooms below the waterline of the ship, so that's where I headed. Or at least that's where I hoped I was headed.

My decision-making skills paid off with the awful

reward of seeing flecks of blood upon the military-clean linoleum. I really hoped this was just carnage from the fight and not vampire drool from mid-snack.

I got down into a more work-a-day-looking area of the boat. No one had bothered to hide the pipes in the ceiling, the beams holding up the roof were unfinished and slathered with sloppy coats of lead paint, and the long hallway was looking a little what one might call ratty. It was pretty clear whoever was occupying this floor didn't place sparkling clean freshness high on the priorities list. It also had that unnerving silence that we found on that floor with the pool. Who knows. I could have actually been on the floor with the pool. I was so lost.

I did, however, get some ideas when the first vampire jumped out at me. He came straight out of one of the doors on the interior side of the boat, leading me to believe these rooms were indeed reserved for fellows who were more night owls than morning larks. Guess he needed a midnight snack and figured the hired help were there to help him help his hunger. He was in for a surprise.

Rather than running for cover, I got him in the heart. He fell to his knees and looked at his chest a little disbelieving. I decided to help him with the reality check. I walked over and kicked it in, deep and good.

Unfortunately, that's when the second vampire came running at me. I felt his arms wrap around my shoulders and try to wrestle me to the ground. I bent and flung him over my head. I planted his skull into the ground with a crunch. I used the momentum to roll over on top of him as I reached over for my stake. This muthafucker was going to die if he wanted to or not.

My balance was off, though, and he flipped me off him and jumped back into the reception area at the end of the hallway. Fine by me. A little more elbow room made things more fun.

Young vampires are kind of a bore. If they're older, they know enough to try some different tricks. But with young vampires, they think they can get by on their good looks and pretty faces. This guy was in for a nasty surprise. I was about to educate him that it was brains over beauty every day.

I ducked as he flew towards me, and popped back up as he miscalculated and went over. I grabbed his feet just as they sailed past my ears and slammed his head into the floor like an ice skater doing a death drop. Except I didn't feel like keeping his face from hitting the ground.

It felt so good, I decided maybe he needed a couple more rides on my swing. I spun around and around, hitting his face on the two steel beams holding the ceiling up. I kept going until his head popped off. Decapitation is a messier way of killing a vampire, but any port in a storm, what have you.

I flung his limp body away, walked over to the dead soldier, and FINALLY got my stake back. I wiped it off on my pants. There were vampire guts everywhere, but that is one of those hazards of the trade.

"KILLIAN!" I called.

Nobody answered back, which meant he was either far away, stuck somewhere and couldn't call back, or stuck somewhere and unconscious. I figured as long as he wasn't dead or undead, we were having a good day.

I took off and found myself entering the galley of the ship. For a boat this size, there should have been meals being prepared night and day. Instead, there was nothing. Made me think that whoever was in charge wasn't planning on having folks around to feed for much longer.

"Killian!" I called out again.

"Killian!" hissed someone back, someone who was most definitely not Killian.

"Oh fuck it." I turned around and there was an older vampire. You can tell because they are uglier. The ease of dispatching them was inversely proportional to the aesthetic appeal of their mugs. And this guy was ugly.

"Mutherfucker," I swore. "What now?"

The vampire came walking slowly at me, which is, in some ways, even scarier than one who rushes you. Tends to indicate that they know what they're doing and are going to be watching your weaknesses for the cue to attack.

"I just want my partner back," I said, holding up my hands as if somehow I could convince him I was just this harmless little girl ready to go her happy way if he played nice.

"He shall die, just as you shall die, Maggie MacKay."

So much for that tactic.

"There is quite a bounty on your head," he continued.

"STILL?!?! I'm pretty sure that got withdrawn when I didn't kill your vampire leader the week before last. An older fellow named Vaclav, maybe you've heard of him."

Name-dropping had just about the same effectiveness rate as when I tried it at some club with a red velvet rope.

"Oh, it would have been withdrawn if you HAD killed Vaclav. I serve another master."

I groaned. "Not another master."

"ANOTHER MASTER!"

"Tell your other fucking master I have had one too many vampire masters for one lifetime. Quit scaring the ghosts away and chomping on passengers and we are even steven and I will get out of your hair!"

"I do not believe he can agree to those terms."

"I think that maybe a jerk like him should reconsider," I said as I grabbed a pan and hurled it, hoping to distract him enough to make a move. No such luck. He just batted it away and kept coming.

"And why should he reconsider?"

"Because otherwise I'm going to kill him."

The vampire began to laugh. Vampire laughs are awful things. It's like all the joy is sucked out of the room and replaced with pictures of crying velvet clowns. Creepy and not the least bit funny.

"Maggie, prepare for your own death!"

"Sorry, dude. I'm afraid that is not on my cruise schedule."

I ran at him with my stake. He dodged out of the way and leapt over my head, landing behind me. Kind of like the move his friend had just executed, except with more finesse.

"How many of you are on this boat?" I asked.

"Hundreds! And there will be hundreds more!"

"Where are 'hundreds more' coming from?"

"You don't know, Maggie MacKay, do you?"

"If I knew, I wouldn't be asking, dumbass."

"When the third whistle of the boat's bell rings, the boundary shall be torn down!" He grinned, thoroughly pleased with himself that it looked like he had ruined my day.

"Oh. No, I knew about that."

That took the wind out of his sails.

"Armageddon comes down upon our heads at midnight, right?"

"Who told you?" he spat as he came at me.

I jumped out of the way. "You think I wouldn't figure it out? I am not just some dumb world walker that stumbled into your little time bubble. I am a MacKay."

"Well, then, Maggie MacKay, prepare for your doom!"

"Listen, if you're going to kill me, can my last request be that you shut the hell up and get on with it?"

"Oh Maggie, I do not intend to kill you," he replied. "You would be a valuable catch for our clan."

You know how it feels when some gross guy leers at you at a bar? He hasn't done anything, but just him breathing makes you want to take a Silkwood shower? That's the way this guy made me feel.

"Sorry, I'm afraid I'm not going to allow you to take me alive," I replied.

"Well, finally we have something to battle for, don't we? Funny that I shall be fighting for your life while you seek your death."

"Just another Saturday in my world," I replied.

I heard a tap-tap-tap on a pipe above my head.

"Killian," I whispered.

While my head was turned, the vampire took off

towards me.

Here's the thing: this guy was smart, but not that smart. Did he really think I would be distracted by fucking Morse code? You hear Morse code. You don't see it. I held my ground until he was almost on top of me and then braced the blunt end of the stake against my heart as he fell upon me.

The pointy end was his direction.

I pushed him off me and he dropped lifelessly to the ground. "Well, I know you are tearing down the boundary, I've got until midnight, and you want me alive. Thank you for your time." I looked down at his lifeless body. "Health inspector isn't going to be too pleased about this sort of kitchen contamination." I kicked him under the counter before turning back to the pipe and tapping, "You safe, partner?"

"Yes," came back the reply.

"Where you at?"

I waited a few moments before the tapping returned.

"Dark."

Fuck. He was in the dark. Nothing like getting yourself kidnapped and then not knowing where you were to screw up your rescue operation.

"Any other clues?" I asked.

"Hurt," was all that replied.

I cussed.

"Don't die," I replied. And I meant it. "Keep banging."

I ran off towards the sound and hoped that no one else was off running, too.

There was a moment when the echoes got me a little confused, but then I followed them across a catwalk and into another cavernous room. At first, I

134

thought it was the same cavernous room we had been in before, the one with the massive legion of vampires and the scary huge portal, but this one must have been on the other end of the boat. Otherwise, it looked exactly like the other cavernous room - raw and unfinished. Walls of steel. Probably someplace to stick some cargo or some ballasts.

It was dark, though. Very, very dark.

"Killian!" I called.

I heard a soft noise from far below.

If that fucking elf died before I got to him, I swear to God I was going to kill him.

I ran down the stairs and found myself looking at a big, flat platform. Must've been at least fifty by fifty feet, not that I could even see where it ended. Way off in the distance, I thought I saw a door that looked like it could have been the engine room. The platform was huge, though, and evened out the v-shaped bottom of the boat so that folks could walk from one end of the room to the other without rolling downhill and taking a dip in the bilge water. In the middle of the platform, though, was a gaping hole that had an eerie blue light glowing out of it. It was about as strong as a bathroom light sneaking through the cracks of the door. There were little catwalks that wrapped around the edge of the hole and the edge of the larger platform. They skirted over the beams and uneven floor joints. You had to run across the catwalk in order to get to the platform, which seemed like an accident waiting to happen. But like I had anything better to do.

I didn't see the vampire come, I felt it. It was just so fucking dark. I wished to God I had some light. I kicked it as it grabbed at my ankle.

"Killian!" I yelled as I stomped on another set of fingers.

"Here Maggie!" he yelled.

"Did you pack a flashlight, Killian? Or some fire?" I yelled as I put my foot between the vampire's body and my own. I pushed him off. Not that moves like that did much damage. The vampire just flew away. The end. Gravity wasn't working in my favor.

I got out my stake. It was like playing 7 Minutes in Heaven in a dark closet in middle school with some guy who was all hands, only this guy was also all fangs. I'd feel his hand on my waist, and by the time I turned, he was out of striking distance. I felt his teeth bang against my collar and once again thanked the lucky stars I wore it. I felt him ripping at my dress, his claws using my Kevlar like a pin cushion. I figured as long as I kept running towards that blue light, it would get easier to see what I was doing. His goal seemed to be in direct opposition to that. He had been good about keeping quiet and sticking to the shadows, but then he stepped in between the light and me and I took the opportunity to play a little pin-the-stake-on-the-vampire.

I paused for a minute just to catch my breath as he dropped. I kicked his body off the side of the catwalk. He scraped up my arms something fierce and I probably could use a Band-Aid or two, but still... it had been too easy. He could have picked me up. He could have knocked me silly. Instead, he made me look at that blue light like it was some sort of homing beacon that I should run to with wide open arms, like a 70's chick on the beach.

"Maggie?" came a weak voice.

No matter what I was feeling, that voice cut

through all rationality and/or bullshit.

"Killian? I'm coming!" I said.

I crept forward carefully. There seemed to be some sort of force field dancing across the top of the hole. In the middle of the hole, down in the pointy part of the bottom of the boat, was my partner. He had been tapping out his Morse code by knocking his messages into the hull with his staff.

"Killian!" I shouted.

He looked up.

He was being used as bait for me. I could tell. They wouldn't have kept him alive otherwise. They wanted me to break through that boundary and probably get caught in the same vortex of hell that they had imprisoned him in.

"Maggie..." he whispered.

There are times when it is tough to know what to do. Do you risk the whole world to save a single life? Or do you destroy a person to ensure the survival of the world? Mortimer was somewhere upstairs getting ready to play an organ that would pull down the boundary between Earth and The Other Side. My grandmother needed to get back into the past so that I could be born. And yet? Call me a sap, but when it comes to Killian, the world was on its own.

I didn't get a choice in proving my loyalties, though, because as I sat there figuring out the hierarchical structure of the universe, I felt hands on my back and a great big push. I fell through the force field and got a little zap. Okay, so it was a big old zap. The entire place seemed to explode around me. I saw stars flash before my eyes. My entire body felt like it was jello. I collapsed on the ground. I felt like toast. I felt like someone had put me in a great big oven and left me to bake at 425 for thirty minutes. I groaned.

"Oh, fuck, Killian."

He picked up his head and looked at me. "You came."

I looked up. The vampire's face peered over the edge of the hole. Guess I wasn't as good as I thought I was. Juice from where I staked him dripped down onto the top of the force field, sizzling with contact. The vampire smiled and then disappeared. No need to let Killian know a vampire got a jump on me. "Damned straight I came. What the hell have you gotten us into?"

"I suppose the heroic thing to say at this moment would be that you shouldn't have come."

"Don't go telling me things I'm figuring out for myself."

"But I am very glad you came."

I punched him softly in the arm. "I know." I looked around the room. "So how are we going to get out of this place?"

Killian shrugged softly, "I don't know. I tried to escape through the field and this is what happened to me." He pointed at some singe marks on his hands. "The field seems to feed off of its captive's energy and use it to strengthen itself. There doesn't appear to be any way out." He clarified. "There is no way out."

"You could have told me this before I came in."

"I was busy trying not to die, as per your instruction."

I picked myself up and felt my way around the hole. I didn't feel any weakness.

"Have you been having a lovely evening, Maggie?"

Killian asked.

"It's been a hoot and a half. Found out at midnight, the walls come down and they turn me into a vampire."

"Oh. Another Saturday night."

The platform was at least ten feet above us. There weren't any walls to scale, just a great big force field that was happy to zap me like a kid pissing on an electric fence.

"I told you so," Killian said.

"Shut up, Killian."

I looked around. "Okay, so if it was electric, that means there is a circuit. We just have to break the circuit. How hard can that be?"

"Hard."

"Shut up." I looked around. "Okay, so circuit... break the circuit... We need something plastic."

"We're in the middle of a steel ship. There is no plastic."

"Quit pointing out the obvious, Killian."

"Can you make a portal?"

That was Killian's answer to everything. I sighed and reached out to push through the boundary. Looks like the vampires thought of everything.

"Nope."

"So we sit and wait for the world to end?"

"I think so."

"Want to make out?"

I looked at Killian, "NO."

"If we are about to bridge the gap between half-dead and all-dead, we could at least make it enjoyable..."

"Listen bucko, this might be your last moments, but I've got an eternity of sucking on necks to look forward to."

"Lucky girl," he said, lying back down.

I went over and rubbed his chest. "Come on, elf. Keep fighting. We'll get out of this."

"I would like to sleep forever," he said, his eyes drifting closed.

"What? The vampires keeping you up past your bedtime?" I asked.

"Someday, I shall keep you up past your bedtime, Maggie," he murmured.

"You must have fallen asleep, because you're dreaming."

He gave me a drowsy little, "Mmmhmmm. How much more time until the next whistle blows?"

I looked down at my watch. "Fifteen minutes."

He closed his eyes. "Awake me in ten."

Just then, there was a light that started to glow in the far end of the bow of the ship. The sound of someone whistling a merry tune echoed through the cavern of metal. And there was Mortimer. Fucking Mortimer! Strolling into the place like a Sunday in the park.

I sat up.

"No, come back," said Killian.

"It's Mortimer," I said, pointing at everyone's favorite idiot musician. "I have to warn him." I walked over to the edge of the force field. "Go back!" I shouted. "It's a trap!"

He wasn't listening. He just kept walking towards us and whistling, even as I kept waving him away. "It's a trap! A trap! Get out! You can't—"

He walked straight up to the force field, playing absolutely no attention to me. He looked it up and down. And then he started singing *Twinkle Twinkle*.

140

The moment the sound of his voice hit the field, it parted it like an umbrella in a waterfall.

I guess it made sense. This siren could tinkle the ivories and bring down the entire border between Earth and The Other Side. It was probably not too much of a stretch to think his voice could part a little boundary made by a bunch of stupid vampires.

But then the dummy walked inside and was trapped in the bubble right along with us. I looked up and six vampire heads popped over the top of the hole. They were so happy, you'd think their favorite team won the Super Bowl.

"Shouldn't you be trapped by a psychovampiric world walker and chained to an organ somewhere?" I asked Mortimer.

He shrugged. "I forgot my sheet music."

"You were supposed to get us out, not come in," I groaned.

"Maggie, this is the safest place to be on this ship!" he pointed out with a great deal of insistence. "Did you know there are vampires on every floor?"

"Really?" I replied, pointing at all of the drooling vampires on the platform overhead.

Mortimer's face became cross. "How is an artist supposed to work with this sort of attention," he grumbled. He began to whistle again. The vampires seemed confused, disoriented, like they couldn't see us below.

"Are you doing that?" I asked.

Mortimer stopped. The moment he did, the vampires were back on us, tracking us like cats in front of a fishbowl.

"A siren's music is their source of greatest pride," he replied.

A plan started formulating in my head. "Okay... OKAY! So can you sing us out of this bubble and hide our movements with your whistling?"

He sighed like I had asked Mozart to play chopsticks. "If that is really what you want..."

"Yes, yes, that is EXACTLY what I want." I put my arm under Killian's shoulder and lifted him gently. He was about as cooperative as a sack of potatoes. "Come on. Support your own weight, Killian."

"I am."

I hiked him higher on my shoulders and turned to the siren. "Okay, Mortimer. Sing loud and sing proud."

"I play the organ."

"Whatever. You know what I mean."

He walked back over to the edge and ran his fingers through his hair. He fixed his cuffs. He straightened his jacket.

"Get on with it!" I said.

"I have an audience," he replied, pointing out the undead watching us from above. "I will not compromise my artistic values for the sake of speed."

"For God's sake," I muttered.

"You are only as good as your last performance!" he said with a great flourish of his arms.

"IF YOU DON'T SPEED THIS UP THIS WILL BE YOUR LAST PERFORMANCE!"

He gave me a dirty look, cleared his throat, and started up another stirring rendition of *Twinkle Twinkle*.

The bubble parted and I dragged Killian through. I was so grateful to be back in the darkness of the middle of that boat. Mortimer strode through like Pavarotti taking center stage. The vampires started hissing like vipers and were jumping off the platform to take us down.

"START WHISTLING!" I shouted. "WHISTLE!"

Mortimer sighed, put his lips together, and blew. The vampires stopped in their tracks. They looked around, as if absolutely confused by why they were here.

Killian jerked his head towards the direction Mortimer original came. "Go that way, Maggie."

I dragged him along, Mortimer marching along behind with happy little head bobs and wrist-flicks to whatever tune he was improvising.

I could see the steps ahead of us leading to the engine room.

"This is good!" I said. "I mean, I have no idea where anything else is compared to here, but I recognize this spot!"

"Good," Killian murmured, fading in and out a little.

"Killian, I promise if you keep fighting, I will let you take me to my first midsummer dance."

"I thought you wanted to inspire me to live, Maggie."

Sarcasm. The elf was going to be alright.

"Killian, we have the organist. We escaped the time-bubble trap. Let's say we go destroy this instrument of doom and wrap this party up."

Killian gave me a thumbs up.

And that's when Mortimer's music stopped. I turned back to look at him. "Why did you stop?!?"

He stroked his throat. "I am parched. Perhaps if we can find a glass of water I can continue. By the way, Maggie, do you think you could help me find my sheet music?"

I looked back where we had come. The vampires were backlit by the blue bubble and were headed our way.

"Sure, Mortimer," I gulped. "I'm pretty sure it is up these steps."

And then I hauled ass, pulling Killian up through the door to the engine room.

CHAPTER NINETEEN

"Come on," I said, pointing towards the end of the engine room. "Let's get up to the pool so that we can push Mortimer through to the future and hopefully skip this whole mess."

I hoped that I was grievously overestimating vampire brain power and that they thought there was no possible way we could escape our prison.

Note to self: With this crew, discontinue the Underestimating-Brain-Power Plan.

We were halfway through the engine room, limping along the gangplank, when there was suddenly the sound of metal slamming on metal.

I guess the vampires' failsafe was that if Killian and/or I and/or whoever else escaped, they'd trap us here. The water-tight door behind us slammed shut and the water-tight door in front of us was starting to close, too. On the other side of the closing door ahead of us was a vampire, there to make sure we didn't get through.

Killian and I didn't even hesitate. With a burst of energy I didn't even know Killian had in him, we both ran full tilt towards that door. Mortimer took up the rear, but I figured they needed Mortimer. Mortimer was probably on the Do Not Kill List. And a few minutes locked away safely in a room was not necessarily the worst thing in the world for a guy like him.

We all got through just in the nick of time. I mowed straight into that vampire like a linebacker, because unlike some of the other members of our team, I was wearing enough protection to take a direct hit to the throat. And he totally tried to directly throat me.

I shouted, "Keep going, I'm coming!" as the vampire and I rolled around. Mortimer helped Killian vault over and keep running.

"Why do they keep trying to kill me?" Mortimer whined. "I am happy to share my music! There is no need for this violence..."

I jumped up to go, but the vampire grabbed my ankle. I kicked him in the head and headed myself for the next door. I got there just in time as the door slammed shut. The vampire started pounding on the metal, but eighteen inches of steel said he wasn't going anywhere. Seriously, if those vampires had stuck Killian and I in one of these rooms in the first place, we would probably still be sitting there.

There was another vampire in this room that Killian was dispatching. Even in his half- dead, beat up state, Killian managed to knife that guy right through the heart. I couldn't help beaming with pride. That was my partner.

Killian held his hand out to me and shouted,

"Maggie! Hurry!"

Like I needed a reminder.

We all got through the next door. I guess the vampire inside was trying to be tricky or something, though, because he hid himself and came at us from behind. Killian and I turned the moment we heard him. The door started to close. I lifted up one of my size ten boots and gave the vampire a kick. The door closed square on his chest.

"Door 13," I remarked. "Your lucky number."

The vampire was bisected, which was good. He wasn't dead, mind you. Just squished in two.

He hissed at me, "So you've returned to finish our battle, Maggie MacKay. Come over here so that I might finish you."

Some people like fluffy bunnies, I have a thing for monsters who are completely lost causes and continue to fight. You gotta admire their gumption.

Killian walked over and staked him through the heart.

"Hey! What the fuck, Killian! I was going to keep him."

"He would not have gotten along with your cat."

"You have a point."

"I think that vampire has the point," Killian said.

The elf was definitely feeling better.

"Come on, you," I laughed.

Suddenly I heard a loud "thunk" and the sound of a watermelon getting dropped on the floor.

Jackie was standing there on the catwalk with the wrench and a fierce look on her face. Down below, George was making short work of a vampire. He was like a Rottweiler with a chew toy.

"Did you do that?" I asked Jackie, pointing at the

vampire.

"I told you I could help!" she said with a grin.

George finished off the guy and looked up at us. "Sorry, Maggie! They attacked us on the other end. We were only able to get this one, but they got your guy in the fancy suit."

"Mortimer?" I said. I turned around and then realized what was going on. Mortimer was gone. Arguably the most important person in our party was now missing and the vampires had the one thing they needed in order to get their party started.

I looked around the engine room, "This better not be the day the music dies..."

CHAPTER TWENTY

"How up are you for running, Killian?" I asked him.

He straightened himself out. "At your service, Maggie."

But he was limping at a slow half-jog, which didn't bode well. Even though the entire world was sort of hanging in the balance and I could have used an extra hand, I knew the vampires would finish him off before we ever got a chance to save the world. And truth be told, if Killian died, there wasn't much of a world left worth saving. Not that I would ever say that aloud to that fucking elf.

I turned to George. "George? I need you to watch one more person for me."

Killian tried to stop me, but I shut him down before he could say a word. "Listen, partner. I know you want to go all macho on me, but I know you elves. Given a couple minutes to rest, you'll be on your feet in no time flat. If you keep pushing, I'm going to be scraping your dead body off of a

149

bulkhead. And that's a hassle."

He opened his mouth again to protest, but Jackie came over and took his hand. "Can you protect me?" she asked.

Leave it to a MacKay girl to figure out how to wrap an elf around her little finger.

Killian looked down at her and then looked at me. "Did you instigate this?"

I shook my head. "Nope, the kid needs you all on her own. You wouldn't go disappointing a child now, would you?"

Jackie gave him a low, slow blink with her big ol' eyes. Killian sighed, utterly defeated. The girl was a player.

"So this power over males is genetic, is it not, Maggie?"

I gave him a shrug. "What can I say? Us MacKay women got skilz." I came over and hugged Killian. "Rest. I'll be back as soon as I get Mortimer. I promise."

He hugged me back. "I will hold you to that."

I turned, ready to go. Then, I stopped and turned slowly back to Killian, unsure of whether to speak.

"What is it, Maggie?" he asked tenderly.

"Killian?"

"Yes?"

"Which direction should I go?"

CHAPTER TWENTY-ONE

Killian drew me a map, which made this stumbling around in the boat thing a whole heck of a lot easier. I mean, yes, it made it a little harder to keep my eyeballs peeled for vampires, but I handled the few I ran into well enough that I barely lost my place.

I certainly was not what you might call "thrilled to pieces" about having to go this alone, but it wasn't so different than what life was like those two years that my dad was caught in the boundary. I mean, of course I was caught on a ship with a boatload of undead things, but still. I had gone it alone for a long time and tried to tell myself I didn't need that pain in the ass elf by my side, anyways.

That's what I told myself.

I was so distracted by all of the layers of dimensions that I practically stumbled into the organ room and the two vampire soldiers standing guard. I ducked back around the corner before they saw me. I folded up my map and tucked it down my front.

Figured it wouldn't ruin the lines of my dress any worse than my monster-proof vest. And this maid's outfit was so shot to hell, there wasn't much left to ruin anyways.

I pulled out my silver stake and my more utility stake, took a deep breath, and ran.

These fuckers weren't messing around. I guess I had screwed up their plans enough that they were willing to take me out now, even if it took them out, too. They pulled out some WWII standard issue handguns and started firing. I took a bullet to the shoulder that felt like a mule kicked me in the collar bone. I took another hit to the stomach that knocked the wind right out of me and dropped me to the ground.

The fact they were young vampires, and more apt to think with their fangs than their heads, was the only thing that saved me. Me flopping around on the ground like some sort of wounded animal was like dancing a laser beam in front of a cat. They tossed their guns aside and sprang, ready for lunch. I tried not to think about the fact, too, that if I was dying and their master was keen on turning me, someone had to do the turning part before my heart stopped beating. They started pushing each other to see who was going to have the honor of hitting my carotid first, and while they were distracted, I had the time to pull a little derringer out of my boot top and nail them at close range. I made sure to give them an extra poke through the sternum to make sure they weren't coming back. And maybe an extra kick or two to their heads, just for being assholes.

I limped off down the hall, each breath feeling a bit like someone got a knife in me. I don't think anything was broken, but my ribs were going to be sporting some nasty bruises for the next couple of weeks. Fucking vampires.

I pushed open the door.

Two vampires had Mortimer held down in his chair and had his fingers pressed to the keyboards.

"PLAY!" Barbara screamed at him.

"I do not feel inspired!" he shouted back.

His poor feet were bleeding all over the foot pedals and those magic spikes were sporting a new coat of rust-colored paint.

Everyone stopped and looked at me.

"Fuck," I said. I so was not feeling this right now. I shot my stake at one of the vampires before he could move and dropped him on the spot. I waved my remaining stake at the other guy. "Come on. Let's get this over with," I groaned.

"You came, Maggie!" said Mortimer. "Finally! An audience who appreciates my work as a musician and who doesn't treat me like some Tin Pan Alley player."

"I've always believed in you!" I said as Barbara and the remaining vampire squared off with me. Two vampires and one stake. It was enough to make anyone want to throw up.

They both flew at me at once, and all I could manage was to hit some defensive postures. I wished to God Killian had packed some of that medicinal healing elf nectar I had tasted a couple times. We needed to start carrying old-skool thermoses of that stuff. I was getting beat and beat bad. I was hoping that eventually the adrenaline would kick in enough to dull out the pain, but it wasn't happening quick enough. I wasn't able to do much more than be their punching bag and hope eventually they'd get bored.

"Stop it!" Mortimer yelled as I took a punch to the jaw that had me seeing stars.

"Play the organ!" shouted back Barbara.

"Leave her be and I will play all you want!"

The other vampire grabbed my arms and had me pinned, holding me there for Barbara to do her worst. I managed to get my foot around his ankle and kick his leg out from under him, but didn't know if I was going to have the energy to flip him over my head.

Mortimer didn't give me a chance to figure that out though. He pressed his fingers on the organ in the ugliest sounding chord of discordant notes ever played by a middle school band. The noise that came out of the organ was like standing in front of a jet plane. The sound knocked all of us onto our butts. It wasn't just sound. It was raw, inter-dimensional power being ripped apart as worlds were forced to collide. It rumbled through the steel of the ship and I could hear it pour out of the smokestack. My ears were still ringing long after the sound had faded away.

Barbara grabbed Mortimer and yanked him to his feet. The other vampire looked like he wanted to have another go at me, but Barbara snapped at him, "Leave it!" and he slunk after her like a pit bull on a choke chain. I was only too happy to let him go. Sometimes you need to know when to stay down, and I needed to stay down.

The thing that got me was Mortimer, though. His steps left puddles of blood as he followed her in tow, the organ having claimed its price of admission.

As they walked past, he just whispered to me, "My apologies."

I couldn't help it. I shouted at them just as they reached the door, "Aren't you going to finish me off?"

I struggled up to my feet.

Barbara smiled. "Never fear, Maggie. I shall make sure you are well attended to."

"If you hurt her, I will not play again!" said Mortimer.

She tutted at him, "Now, Mortimer. I will do no such thing. Maggie will rest comfortably here in 1941 and watch the years pass comfortably by."

I suddenly understood what she was doing. She wasn't going to kill me. She was going to trap me in this bubble of time and when it blinked out, so would I. Or, more accurately, I'd be stuck here traveling along this timeline as the years and decades passed and get to look forward to spending my golden years in the 1980's.

Fuck that shit.

No one should have to live through the 1980's again.

I hobbled after them, making sure to stay out of sight, but looking for any opportunity to take them down without giving them an opportunity to return the favor.

I was SOL.

They went into the pool room. I opened up the door just enough to see them. The waters were still filled with their bathing beauties and I had no idea when they'd decide that dinner was served.

Barbara jumped through the portal with Mortimer in tow. There was an instant, a split second when I could have followed after them, but then I thought of Killian and Jackie down in the engine room and I couldn't do it. Even with the fate of the world hanging in the balance, I couldn't do it.

I looked at the boundary as it slowly closed in

front of me, almost taunting me to jump on through, but all I could think of was that time I had jumped through and left my dad caught in limbo-land. Sure, he wanted to get caught, and sure, we got him out later... But I couldn't go through something like that again. If this reality blinked out, or worse, Killian ended up storming the shores of Normandy... It just wasn't cool. I knew the only chance he and Jackie had to make it through was me, and I wasn't going to fuck that up all because a couple of worlds needed saving.

I pulled out my map. I needed to get to Killian. If we never figured out how to reopen the time portal, well... we would just pick up some new hobbies. Swing dancing and maybe in a couple years, doo wop and staking vampires at the car hop.

CHAPTER TWENTY-TWO

I got back down to the engine room. My motley crew was busy playing some sort of game involving throwing wrenches. I think Jackie was winning.

Killian looked up. "I felt it," he said.

Nothing more needed to be said.

But who was I to let a moment like that hang out in thin air? "They grabbed Mortimer and pulled him through the swimming portal. Barbara closed up the door. I didn't want to go through without you guys... just in case I couldn't get back."

"Can we get through now?" he asked.

"No. We're trapped in the bubble."

He threw his wrench with probably a little more force than necessarily necessary for wrench throwing. It hit one of the pipes and the clanging sound clanged something in my brain.

"Wait." I said. I pointed at the pipes. "The smokestacks have to go off in order for all of this to work."

"Yes," Killian affirmed.

"No! You don't get it! The smokestacks have to go off in order for this to work!" I shouted.

"Saying it louder does not increase my understanding, Maggie."

"Mortimer said that his notes have to play simultaneously across three dimensions in three different times in order for the portals to open. So what would happen if we fucked that up?"

"How?"

"What if there was no steam?" I looked over at George. "We stop the steam, we stop the smokestack, we stop the end of the world..."

The gargoyle stood there thinking for a minute, and then a great big smile spread across his ugly horned face. He slowly shook his wrench at me. "Maggie, you might have something there."

We all ran over to one of the boilers.

"How are we going to keep this thing from going off?" I asked.

Killian shook his head. The entire room was made of steel. There was no "For a good time, puncture here" written anywhere.

"Okay, boilers explode all the time," I said. "What we need is something to break through the boiler, like... bullets or something."

"Bullets? You are proposing firing off rounds of shells at a steel object in an enclosed space?" clarified Killian.

"I said LIKE bullets. You come up with something."

We all stood there for a moment.

George rubbed his nose. "I can release the steam, but it will boil all of you humans like lobsters in a pot."

I looked at him. "Will it hurt you?"

He shrugged his shoulders. "We gargoyles are tough. We're made for casting demons into the pits of the Dark Dimension. A little steam will be like a day at a sauna."

I wasn't sure if he actually meant it or was just trying to throw me off so that I would convince him that we'd figure something else out.

"Okay, George," I said walking over to him. "Sabotage the steam here, but we need you to sabotage the steam sixty years from now, too. It is the same night you meet Killian and I in the future. We meet you in the engine room during a ghost tour. I catch you wiping grease on a tourist's leg. You screw up when Jackie tries to get me a message written in soap bubbles and that's why you're in the right place at the right time."

"I'll make sure I get that leg nice and greasy," he said, giving me a three-fingered salute and a wink. "It's like I was put here just for this mission."

I nodded my head. "Okay, kids, let's evacuate the engine room." I held out my hand. "Thanks, George. If you ever need a favor..."

"Know anyone in The Other Side permit department?" he asked.

"I most certainly do," I said. "And as soon as we get home, I will make sure you get to stay here for as long as you feel like."

"Actually, I was hoping for maybe a reassignment. Something with a bit more excitement than this old boat."

"You got yourself a deal. Something nice and close to a hellhole," I said. "Oh! If you fall asleep in the chapel, watch out for kids with permanent markers!"

He gave me a smart salute and scampered off. Killian gave me a little side hug and I winced.

"Are you all right?" he asked, concerned.

I shrugged. "Just ran into a little trouble and realized how much I appreciate it when you're around to distract the gun fire."

We were the walking wounded trying to hobble out of a burning building. It just flat out sucked that neither of us were operating on full steam, so to speak. Jackie probably was the best equipped of our entire crew to take out any bad guys, and she was just a kid with a wrench.

We walked up the steps as the final watertight door sealed behind us. That was that. It was all on George now. I started rubbing my chin, a nagging little thought messing with my head.

"Maggie? What's going on in that head of yours?" Killian asked.

I looked back where we had come from. "Just wondering if we should make sure we have a failsafe in case this doesn't work."

"Why wouldn't it work?" Killian asked.

"It's the future," I said. "How could smokestacks go off in the future if there is no steam to release? The boat is docked. It is a floating hotel. The most steam they have is from their shower room."

I could see Killian was troubled by my thinking, too. My dumb brain and its logic ruining a perfectly good sense of victory.

"Okay, this is okay," I said as we reached the next landing. "What does the steam do?"

"It propels the sound."

160

"So if the sound is wrong..."

"Then the harmonic resonance will not shatter the boundary and the portal doesn't open!" Killian said.

"And you completely fuck their plans!" piped up Jackie.

Killian and I looked at one another and then at the kid.

"You corrupted your own grandmother, Maggie," said Killian, aghast.

"Maybe she's who I get it from," I pointed out, trying not to feel bad.

Jackie giggled, "Nope!" and ran ahead. "Come on!"

We'd have to worry about how much psychological damage we were doing after we finished saving the world, I guess.

"Okay," I said. "Let's get to the roof and see if we can sabotage the smokestacks."

"How would you suggest we do that?" asked Killian.

"Well, we have a boat full of soldiers, heavy equipment, and military supplies," I replied.

We also, evidently, had a boat with a cranky vampire.

Blocking the top of the staircase and our way to the deck was the woman in black.

"Wait. You're supposed to be in the future!" I said.

She started advancing slowly towards us, her silk black dress and flapping in the breeze. "I know all about what you are trying to do," she said.

I pushed Killian and Jackie behind me. "And how did you find out about that?"

"A little gargoyle told me."

"George..." I whispered, having a really bad feeling about this.

"Don't worry. I made sure his death was swift and quick," she replied.

"You're gonna die for hurting my friend," I informed her.

She smiled. "Oh, sweetheart, I'm already dead."

And then she raced down the stairs towards us.

"Killian, get Jackie to safety," I said, pushing them away.

"I cannot leave you, Maggie," he said, his eyes on Barbara as she reached the bottom of the steps.

"Go do what you do best. Find the deck while I keep her distracted," I said.

"Maggie..."

"I'll just get us lost if you leave the 'find the deck' up to me. Go! I'm taking this bitch down."

Killian grabbed the kid's hand and they ran off down the hallway.

"We're not going to let you tear down the boundary," I said, blocking her claws and throwing her to the ground.

She landed like she was resting on a chaise lounge and I was asking her if she preferred lemonade or iced tea. She laughed. "Aren't you quite darling? I don't need to your permission, Maggie MacKay."

"I think you do," I said.

"What are you going to do to stop me?" she pouted.

"I'm going to kill you," I replied, taking out my stake and twirling it in my fingers.

She flew toward me and I sidestepped her. She might look like a kitten, but she fought like a tomcat. Girl vampires fight dirty. She hissed and snarled as she came at me, a flying ball of fangs and claws. I flung her off me and raced up the stairs. She tried to tackle me, but I kicked her in her pretty nose and kept going.

I emerged out onto the deck of the ship, which was a surprise to me. I had no idea we were so close to topside. She hit me again and I tucked and rolled, springing to my feet and trying not to vomit as the pain from earlier decided to let me know it did not appreciate this workout. But the clock was running down. It was dangerously close to midnight and that final whistle.

I looked up to the upper deck. The smokestacks were right in front of me. So close. I was so flipping close to them.

Barbara landed on my back and was biting on my neck guard like a toddler with a teething ring. I slammed her against the railing. Guess a metal bar to the spinal cord isn't the best feeling in the world because she let go.

And I took that opportunity to run. I looked over my shoulder and she was right behind me. But I had a sliver of a plan. It all depended on if I could get America's finest to play along.

"Come and get me, bitch!" I shouted.

"I shall finish you!" she cried.

"I'd like to see you try."

I ran along the deck, dodging between curious soldiers. You could feel the waves of disbelief. I think I had them on my side, though, because I at least tried to weave around them, while Barbara was knocking them down.

"Help! Help!" I cried. Sometimes you gotta work the helpless female angle. The fact Barbara was vamping it up, not in the good way, was working in my favor. The soldiers' disbelief was switching to outright hostility. Over on the left-hand side was a set of stairs which ran up to the upper deck right next to those smokestacks. I took them two at a time. When I reached the top, I turned and she flew at me, not even bothering with the stairs at all. I caught her and dropped down, flipping her over my head. She landed crouched in a three-point position like a linebacker. Truth be told, she could take a hit with the best of them.

"You are going to be my lunch," she hissed.

"Not a chance in hell," I replied.

I ran as she flew again and rolled right under her feet. She landed again and then was chasing behind me.

"Spy!" I shouted at the soldiers on the lower decks, the ones manning the massive deck guns. "She's a Nazi spy!"

Our soldiers might not have known what to do with two women in a catfight and/or a vampire, but they sure as hell knew what to do with one of Hitler's minions. Every soldier had his gun out and was taking aim.

"Shoot her! Shoot her!" came a shout. It sounded like Killian. "Strafe away, men! Stop the fascists in their tracks!"

I dropped down.

The vampire jumped and for a moment Barbara was silhouetted against the smokestack.

"Open fire!" came the cry again.

And then I heard that blessed rat-a-tat-tat. The beautiful sounds of old-timey machine guns and a bona fide Gatling gun, ripping through the metal.

God bless boys and their toys. They nailed Barbara like a metal duck in a shooting gallery. But even more importantly, their bullets punctured the smokestacks.

The sound of gunfire stopped.

I stood up and gave a big thumbs-up in my best impression of a USO Pin-up Girl. "Well done, boys!" The maid outfit helped. I limped over to Barbara. She was filled with so many holes, you could drain a pot of spaghetti through her. She wasn't getting up anytime soon, but she was still alive.

"This is not over," she spat at me, her eyes filled with burning hatred.

"Yes," I said, "it is."

And I nailed her through the heart with my silver stake.

It was over.

And then, I let myself fall over. I was so fucking tired. I lay on the deck of the boat as the soldiers came running to see what happened and if I was okay.

Some fetching young GIs hoisted me to my feet and I was more than happy to let them help me over to the railing. I looked down to see who had manned the big guns. Face down and dead on the deck was the gunner, with overly-long canines in his mouth and Killian's pole through his chest. Taking his place at the trigger was Jackie, sporting an army helmet and a fierce little look on her face. She and Killian were high-fiving.

The clock struck midnight.

All three smokestacks went off. One. Two. They were illuminated against the sky and gave off an eerie glow.

The third went off and the tone was all wrong. It was like a slipped finger on the keyboard of an organ.

It was over. It was finally over. Thank fucking God.

"Thanks, grandma!" I yelled.

Jackie gave me a great big grin and a thumbs-up.

"Are you all right, miss?" asked one of the eighteen-year-old kids at my elbow.

"Just fine," I replied.

Killian grabbed Jackie's hand and came running over. He threw his arms around me and twirled me. If I wasn't so fucking thrilled to be alive, I would have probably passed out from the pain. "Ow!"

He let me down and planted a great big kiss on my cheek. "We did it, Maggie!"

To hell with pain, I hugged him right back.

"You two should get married!" said Jackie, smiling at us.

I messed up her hair. "You sound just like my mother."

Killian planted his fists on his waist in a downright Peter Pan stance, looking pleased as punch. "We did it!"

"Not yet," I said.

It was like I cancelled Christmas. His face absolutely dropped. "What else?"

I turned to the GIs next to me. "Can you watch the kid for a second?" I asked.

Jackie scowled. "I just saved your ass. I can take care of myself."

"Listen, when you clean up that potty mouth of yours, old lady, I'll leave you on your own." She scowled at me and I held my hands up, explaining, "What I have to do next comes from the paternal side of the family. I promise, I will be right back."

Jackie wasn't having it. "I'm coming with you!"

The GI saw I was in trouble and saved my butt

one last time. With a cheesy smile and white-bread earnestness, he pointedly stated, "With our gunner out of commission, I need someone here who can man the turret."

That got Jackie's attention. She turned around and her little face lit up like a search light looking for bombers. "I can!"

He grabbed her hand and walked her over to a bench. "But first, let me show you how to clean a rifle." He wasn't letting her anywhere near heavy artillery, bless his heart.

As soon as they were out of hearing range, Killian asked, "What is left unfinished?"

"We've got a hull full of vampire soldiers all dressed up with no place to go," I reminded him.

Killian groaned. "The vampires in the hull..."

"Yep."

We both took a great big, deep breath and headed off.

CHAPTER TWENTY-THREE

We ran into the bowels of the ship and looked off the catwalk at the shitstorm below. There were two portals now, one on either side of the room. In lockstep, the vampires were leaving this world and marching through, assuming that they were heading into the 21st century to take over the world. What we knew that they didn't know, though, was that this second portal was an open door to nowhere. There was no exit. They were all walking straight into the limboland of the boundary.

As the last of the vampire army marched through, I jerked my head in the general down direction. Killian jerked his head in the "you are fucking nuts" direction. I rolled my eyes in the "I know what I'm doing" direction and crept to the stairs.

None of the vampires came back out of the portal. My guess they were all standing around waiting for the next door to open, so that was working for us.

I walked through the vacated room in between the

two portals just to see if my hunch was right. I could hear the quiet echo of Mortimer's note rolling back and forth between the two. It reminded me of listening to the waves of the ocean.

Since this whole time/dimensional portal business was built on sound, specifically Mortimer's sound, all we needed to do was build a standing wave of that note and we could use the resonance of his lovely little organ music to create its own little bubble in time and space that no one could escape from. My job was just to push one of them closer to the other. Easy-peasy.

I stood behind the one portal. On one side of it, it looked like some sort of glitter-sticker of television static. The other, you couldn't even tell it was there. The other was where I needed to focus the last of my energy.

I placed my hand on the backside of the 1940's portal.

"What are you doing, Maggie?" Killian asked.

"You'll see. Let me know when it starts to get loud and things start shaking."

"You are terrifying me, Maggie."

"Rightfully so. You might want to cover your ears."

And I pushed it towards the 1930's portal.

I felt like one of those strong men in those competitions where they move freight trains with their teeth. And exactly that stupid.

"Can I help?" Killian called.

"Might want to set up a hernia operation appointment for me when I get finished," I grunted.

But I kept pushing.

Mortimer's note kept playing, but wasn't bouncing

right. The sound started to reverberate as the feedback started to build. I pushed some more and the bass kicked up a notch as the peaks of the wave grew closer.

"I think you are doing it, Maggie!" Killian called.

"Fan-fucking-tastic!" I yelled back. My arms were screaming at me. My back was screaming at me. And my head felt like it was about to explode.

And then, just like that, the wave hit the harmonics just right, and like an opera singer wailing at a wine glass, the portals shattered and left nothingness in their place.

I fell down, not sure if I wanted to pass out or throw up first. I picked both.

As the world sort of faded in and out of black spots and hazy images, I felt Killian put my arm over his shoulder and drag me to my feet.

"Do you think you can walk?" he asked, his face looking like something out of a funhouse mirror.

"I'm okey-dokey, partner," I wheezed, giving him the thumbs-up before I passed out again.

I woke up upside-down over Killian's shoulder as he jogged down a hallway. Jackie was, for some reason, trotting right beside him. My earlier injuries were very, very angry at me about being upside down.

"I think I'm going to throw up again," I said.

"Try not to," he replied. "We need to get to the swimming pool."

"Little midnight dip?"

"More of a sunrise swim," he replied as he put me down. I did my best to hurl away from his shoes. I wiped my mouth as he steadied me on his arm.

"What's your rush?" I murmured.

"You have been in and out of consciousness for

many hours, Maggie. It is close to dawn."

"Sorry about that."

"Apology not necessary. But in that time, things have been changing."

He opened the door to the swimming pool. The vampire stew was gone. Instead, there were all sorts of scantily-clad men diving in the pool and splashing around.

"Fuck," I said.

"Fornicating under the consent of the king, indeed," Killian replied. "I believe the other timeline is decaying and the boat is returning to its journey on the Atlantic Ocean."

"Double fuck."

"Hey, Nurse! That sure is a funny getup!" one of the guys called out to me.

"Special mission!" I shouted. "Clean up duty."

"Is that your kid? She sure is cute!"

"I'm Jackie! And I saved your ass!" she shouted back. The soldiers just laughed at her spunk.

"Really, we need to talk about this new habit of yours," I said.

One of the soldiers wasn't buying our whole we're-with-the-band act. Guess our bloodstained, ripped uniforms and bruises might have set off some bells and whistles.

"You don't suppose they're Nazi spies?" I heard one of the guys ask another guy in the pool.

The other one replied, "Not sure, private."

I sure hoped they didn't decide to get out of the water to investigate, because the kid didn't need to see any dough boy privates.

I walked over to the dressing area.

"Is the vortex there?" asked Killian.

Time heals all wounds and it also heals vortexes ripped in the boundary by time-traveling vampire world walkers. It wasn't open, but I could feel the weakness. That said, the weakness was growing stronger. I looked down at Jackie. "We gotta take her back or else I never get born," I stated, leaving it unsaid that if we went backwards in time, we'd have two jumps to make to get to the future, all while we were getting sucked through space to another geographic location as this fake reality decayed.

Killian nodded, though, getting the implications of this decision. He reached out and squeezed my hand. "If our fate is to grow old and gray in the past together, it is a future I could live with."

"I'll get us out of this," I said. "I'm not growing old in the past with you."

"Actually, us elves have a much longer life cycle, so you will, indeed, grow old while I retain my boyish good looks."

"Shut up, elf."

I turned my attention to the vortex and stuck out my hands, ready to work my voodoo.

"Do you think you can do it without getting caught between worlds?" Killian asked.

It was a completely legitimate question, but not exactly the one I needed at this particular moment. I shrugged my shoulders. "Listen, you're with the second best world walker in two dimensions. Maybe three. If anyone can do it, I'm it."

"You failed before on the deck of the ship," he said.

"Practice... practice... practice...." I replied. I reached out and pushed against the ether. Usually when you jump through time, it feels like you're

pushing through Silly Putty. But this was cold, biting
cold, so cold it was hot. Or maybe it was just hot.
Something about molecules, speed of light, time-
travel were bumping around in my head. I didn't pay
that much attention to that episode of Mr. Wizard.

I pushed, though, hoping I wasn't going to singe
my skin off, which was a completely rational fear.
World walkers die all the time, and Barbara might
only have been able to do this over and over because
she was already dead.

Just when I thought that I couldn't bear it any
longer, I broke through. I grabbed Killian's hand and
threw him through it ahead of me, grabbed Jackie and
mooshed her through, and I jumped after. The portal
sealed right behind us. It was smoking. My skin
looked like I fell asleep out in the sun and was
instantly blistering. I had brand new respect for that
world walker those vampires had turned. I thought
that she was a slouch because she left a scar on the
dimension. The reason that scar was there was
because she had ripped a hole where there should
never have been one.

"OW!" I said, poking at my skin, watching it go
from red to white back to red.

A woman screamed. I looked up. We had landed
in the ladies' dressing room and this bathing
beauty was sporting a blue wool number that left
everything to the imagination. She shouted again,
"You're a ghost!"

"No," I said, trying to calm her down.
"It's magic."

"You're magic!" she screamed.

I started the verbal tap dance. "Listen, lady, what
are you even doing here? This area is closed."

I completely ignored the fact you could hear a ton of swimmers splashing about in the water outside the stall.

"Why are you magic?" she replied hysterically.

Killian picked it up from there. "We are part of the evening's entertainment. Management told us to practice here."

She blinked. "You're practicing in the first class swimming pool dressing room?"

I took at Killian and Jackie. "Oh, no! Is this the first class swimming pool dressing room? We're supposed to be in the third class swimming pool dressing room. We are in the wrong place. So sorry! Please don't tell anyone! We could get fired."

She nodded slowly and then began to smile as she peered closer. "You really are very good. You had me completely convinced."

"Just smoke and mirrors, lady. Do you really think we'd be wearing costumes like this if we were real?"

I held out my ratty, bloody skirt and gave a little curtsy. Killian pointed at his ears and shook his head as if he wouldn't be caught dead in this getup.

"Well, thank you for the sneak peak!" she bubbled. "I would love to bring my friends to the show tonight. Where will you be playing?"

"In the... ballroom. Tomorrow. At 7 p.m. See you there," and I pushed Killian and Jackie towards the doorway.

"I'll bring my friends!"

"Great! Let's hope they don't change the venue on us like they did last week!" I piped up before we speed-walked out into the hallway.

Killian put his arm around my shoulder and planted a kiss on the top of my head.

"GENTLE! My skin is on fire."

"As is mine around you, Maggie."

"Ew! Gross!" said Jackie.

"Me, too, kid," I replied, hugging Killian back.

CHAPTER TWENTY-FOUR

Jackie stopped in front of the second class nursery door. A nanny holding the hand of a little boy in a sailor suit walked by us. She smiled as she opened the door to the nursery and asked Jackie, "Are you coming in?"

Jackie shook her head. "I just have to say goodbye to my caretakers."

The nanny looked at Killian and me, but had the good grace to not mention we looked like hell. The door closed behind her. Jackie looked around, distracted.

"What is it?" I asked.

She waited for a moment before speaking. "I remember that nanny. She said the same thing before. Only, then there was Barbara and then after that I started seeing all the ghosts." Jackie peered down the hallway. No one came. Jackie smiled. "I guess she isn't coming."

Killian gave me a little atta-girl cuff to the chin. "Not only did you open that time/space portal, you got us here before the vampire time bubble began. We are now in regular time."

I buffed my nails. Not too shabby.

"I should go in," Jackie finally said.

Killian knelt down and gave her a hug. "Thank you."

She let go of him and then ran over to me, throwing her arms around my waist.

With the threat of imminent death behind us, I suddenly realized this wasn't just goodbye... it was goodbye to a woman I had never known in my life. She had been quite a sidekick to our merry band of badasses.

"It was nice to finally meet you, Grandma," I said.

"Will I ever see you again?" she asked, looking up at me and not letting go.

I rested my hand on her head. "Who knows? If we get stuck here, you'll be seeing us all the time."

"But what if you don't get stuck here?"

"You'll see me when I'm little," I replied. "But I really liked getting to meet you now that I am big."

"When I grow up," she said, looking straight up at me, "I want to be like you."

"When you grow up," I assured her, "you turn into someone even better."

"Be happy, Maggie," she said.

I felt my eyes start to prickle and kissed her. "Will do. Now go inside before you get us reported for kidnapping."

She gave me one last squeeze and then went through the door. Killian came over. Silently, he picked up a corner of my apron and offered it to me.

"Fucking allergies," I said, wiping my cheeks.

He gathered me up and just let me rest against him.   "Something is most definitely in bloom," he replied.

CHAPTER TWENTY-FIVE

The corridors were still pretty quiet as all the lazy bones on the boat slept in. I envied them. I could really have used a bed right about now.

"Well, what now?" Killian asked.

"Learn how to jitterbug?" I suggested, dragging my beat ass down the hall.

"I should have left you in the hull of the ship, sunshine," he replied.

"If I had a nickel..."

Killian groaned as he stretched his arms overhead. "I would enjoy a long soak in a hot spring."

"Yes!" I moaned. "Oh, and for a cup of coffee... I sure could use my mom right about now..."

Killian stopped dead. He looked at me first like I was crazy and then like I had gone and reinvented the microchip.

"Your mother!" he shouted. He grabbed me and squeezed me.

"Ooo, careful there, cowboy," I grunted. "I feel like I've been run over by a herd of stampeding buffalos."

"Do you not see?" he asked.

"No."

"The women in your family... You were able to see through the overlapping dimensions. Your grandmother was able to see through the overlapping dimensions. It runs in your maternal genetics, Maggie!"

"But my mom has never been able to see anyone on this boat..."

"That is because the vampires layered false realities over the real one. For the first time in our lives, there is only one timeline upon this location."

I took a second to take that in. The 1930's to present day had all been living on this boat since the 1930's because the vampires had created the bubble. That was not the case anymore. If that was true, then...

I looked around the hallway. We were in the ghost of those vampire time bubbles. We were living in the residual energy left over from them. We were in a ghost bubble. My mom got along GREAT with ghosts.

"Killian, you are BRILLIANT!"

"Deserving of a raise?"

"I will buy you a whole breakfast when we get back to our time, you genius, silly elf!"

He looked around, rubbing his hands. "So, how do we let your mother know?"

"I have no idea."

This was a bit of a pickle. I didn't know that much about ghost bubbles, this being the first time I'd ever heard of or been caught in one, but I knew when ghosts haunted somewhere, they were usually stuck in a location. If we stepped off this ship, we might be stepping into outer space. I had a better chance getting caught in between the boundary and having my dad figure out how to pull us out with that lion statue than mom find us. Somehow we needed to get Mom and Dad over here to the boat.

"Well, the good news is that my mom is neurotic and if I don't check in all week, they'll figure out something is wrong."

"So, we wait for her to track us down?"

I shrugged. "If you have a better idea..."

Killian sat there thinking for a bit, because that dumb elf didn't realize the difference between a rhetorical question and a real one, and then he said, "If only George was still alive..."

I looked at Killian and looked at the direction of the engine room. I let out a huge whoop and flung my arms around that dumb elf's neck. "That's it! Killian, I could kiss you!"

"You could," he confirmed.

"Shut up." I pointed at the engine room. "George! We can save him! He knew us! He knew us in the 1940's. It is because he met us here, in the past, and knew us in the future. He's SUPPOSED to help us. And we are supposed to save him! Come on. We have to reach him before the sun rises. Let's go figure out if we're trapped for all eternity or if the heavens are smiling down on us!"

We took off.

CHAPTER TWENTY-SIX

George was sitting right there in the engine room, pretty as you please.

"George! George the Gargoyle!" I called.

He looked downright flabbergasted that a human would be calling out to him by name. He flashed me his great big fangs and it was all I could do not to turn tail and run. And this is me we're talking about.

"George! Cut it out! You know us!" I said.

He gave me the old stink eye. "I do not believe so, human."

He looked like he was getting ready to take off, so I crossed myself to let him know I wasn't trying to pull anything sneaky on him. "Not now, but we meet you in the future..."

"What sort of cock and bull..." he sputtered.

"Just know that it happens. You don't have to be our buddy now, just know that in the future, we know each other and one day, we are going to show up with a little kid named Jackie and ask you to babysit her for us."

He was still listening. It was pretty clear he wasn't too happy about the fact he was still listening, but he was doing it.

"Just... when that happens, you're going to be asked to help save the world and it is really, really important that you don't do it."

"Why?" he said suspiciously.

"Because you'll die. Tell the bad guys what you're up to, act like you're a double-crossing evil snitch henchman, we'll take it from there, but when we ask you to sabotage steam, it is really important that you let them catch you, and that you don't let them kill you."

"How do I know you're not the bad guys?"

"Wait ten years. You'll see. But we need you to live."

He regarded us, seeming to weigh the weight of our souls. Finally, he nodded. "If what you're saying is true, and I'm not sure I believe you, I appreciate you coming here to save my life."

I didn't want to leave him with the false impression that this was all altruistic. "There's more. After all of this goes down, we, this elf and I, get stuck here in this time. So seventy years from now, we need you to call a man named Father Killarney and tell him to send my mom and dad to the boat. That would be awesome."

I saw George's haunches slowly start to go down. "Did you say a Father Killarney? A priest?"

"Yes, a priest. A man of God. You two get along. He has his own church and everything. In fact, it's your old church. He's the caretaker of your childhood home! On La Brea!"

George sat there a little while longer and said, "Why should I?"

"Because in the future I save your gawddammned—"

Killian put his hand on my arm and reined me back in.

"Because in the future this elf and I save the world, and the only reason we are able to do that is because of that little girl Jackie and you! So it's a full circle kind of thing. And now we need your help so that we can get back home."

George gave me one more suspicious look. "I'll think about it. And if I remember it, maybe I'll do it."

And then he took off up on top of one of the big pipes on the ceiling. And I guess that it must have been morning, because with a great sigh, he turned to rock. And like they say, you can't argue with a stone. I mean, you can, but it isn't like it'll do you much good.

"Okay, Killian. God, I hope George is still alive."

"Do you think he believed us?" Killian asked.

"I'm not taking it for... granite..."

"Maggie? I should have left you in the hull."

CHAPTER TWENTY-SEVEN

Killian and I sat on the deck of the boat, staring at the dock. It was well into mid-morning and still no sign of Mom or Dad. In the distance, the California skyline was getting a hazy cloud of blue to it. This dimensional bubble was collapsing.

"That gargoyle had better not have died..." I said. "God, I hope he listened to us."

"Well, if need be, we shall just go remind him tonight. And tomorrow night. And every single night until he decides to heed our warning and not expire."

"Time is going to catch up with us, Killian," I said, watching the blue nothingness creep. "It started decaying that fake bubble in the 1940's while we were there. You saw what it did. It erased all those vampire soldiers and made things the way they are supposed to be. What if in this thread of time, George doesn't remember what we told him?"

"Except you caught him before the vampire time

bubble began. You brought us back far enough that whatever happens before this moment remains real and true."

"This is making my head hurt."

"Quantum physics can do that to a person."

"What if this doesn't even work and Mom can't even cross us over?"

"It is a ghost ship, Maggie. Your mother, I believe, has connections."

"I hope we can see them," I said, looking out at the barely developed port of Long Beach. Gone were the tourist traps and aquariums and regattas and crazy lighthouses.

"You shall know her, Maggie. She is able to pierce this veil. It is her gift."

And that's when I saw the car. It was like looking at a double exposure film. The parking lot was invisible, so it looked like the car was floating through the hills. I pointed. "There! There she is!"

Killian shook his head, peering at the land. "I don't see it."

"Don't you worry. I'll let you know where to go." I grabbed his hand and pulled him down. "Off to the first class ballroom!"

We dashed down the stairs, pushing our way through slowly moving guests. I didn't even care that we knocked a couple of them down. We were getting out. Down four stories and then we ran the length of the boat. My heart was singing. We were going to go home! Home!

And after everything we'd been through, I had not anticipated the maître d' guarding the ballroom. He closed his reservation book and stepped in front of the door.

"We have to get through," I panted.

He sniffed and looked at my ratty, torn maid costume. "From your attire, I am quite certain you are not guests." He pointed back the way we came. "The entrance for the help is on the other side of the ballroom."

"You don't understand," I said to him. "It is a matter of life and death!"

"I am sorry," he informed me, "but if you do not remove yourself immediately, I shall be forced to fire you without pay and have you forcibly ejected from this boat at the next port of call."

"Sounds perfect." I tried to muscle my way through without actually hurting him, but he wasn't having any of that.

"Stop! Stop! You're making a scene!" he shouted, pushing back.

All of the fancy people in their fancy outfits were giving us a good hard look and whispering not nice things about us.

"This," Killian said, "is bullshit." And with that, he knocked the guy out with a square punch to his jaw. The maître d's eyes rolled back and he keeled over without a fight.

And that was that. We stood looking over him, the entire room hushed in shock.

"My hero," I said, impressed.

Killian placed his hand in the small of my back. "Shall we dance?"

"This time, I'll let you lead," I replied.

We walked into the ballroom. It existed in the double dimension. Tables overlapped. Waiters walked through waiters. But the one thing that cut through and was crystal clear in both worlds was my mom was sitting in the brunch area with Mindy and Dad. Her face turned pale as a sheet as she saw me and Killian.

"What are you doing on that side of the veil? Did you die in a car accident?" she said, jumping to her feet and coming towards us.

Mindy looked at her curiously. She couldn't see us. We were still stuck behind the veil for her eyes.

"Maggie? Killian? Can you talk to me?" Mom asked.

That got Dad's attention. He looked around frantically. "Where are they? Who did this? Who would have gotten Father Killarney to make a call like that?"

"We're fine!" I yelled.

"No need to yell," Mom replied. "I can hear you."

"What did she say?" asked Mindy. "I would know, right? I would know if my twin died, right Mom?"

"She's not dead," Mom answered, then asked us just to make sure, "You're not dead, correct?"

I shook my head. "No, we're just trapped in a time bubble. We were helping out some ghosts."

"Maggie, if you wanted help with ghosts, you should have called. You don't go walking into their world," she chided.

I rolled my eyes. "I know, Mom. I wasn't exactly planning on being here."

She walked around the bubble, feeling it with her hands.

"They're okay, right Mom?" Mindy asked.

Mom nodded, but didn't say anything, I think trying hard not to lose her concentration. She turned to Dad. "They seem to be trapped in some sort of dimension."

Dad looked, but then shook his head. "I can't see them."

"It must be a spirit world," she replied. "I think I should try to cross them over."

Dad looked at her like she was nuts. "Are you sure you won't cross them over to that other place where crossed over ghosts tend to go?"

Mom sighed. "This is worse than that time Maggie got her knee caught in that tree house wall."

Killian looked at me. "Why was your knee caught in a tree house wall?"

"All world walkers go through an awkward stage..." I said.

"Do you have photographs?" he asked.

Mom chuckled. "Oh, I have plenty, Killian. Come over for dinner on Sunday. I'll show you the whole album! You should have seen that terrible perm Maggie thought would look so great."

"If you two don't stop right now, I'm staying on this side of the veil," I threatened.

Mom turned to Dad. "Dear, I just don't know how to get them unstuck."

Dad looked again. "What if I opened up a portal and you called them through?"

Mom thought it over. "I suppose that could work. Maggie? Killian? We're going to try and cross you over." She muttered to herself, "I can't believe they went wandering into a ghost dimension."

"We are standing right here."

"How many times have I told you not to play with ghosts?"

"No times! You always told me to befriend them and have tolerance for the unliving!"

"Being friendly and following them into another

dimension are two entirely different stories, young lady."

"Just get me out of this and you can yell at me all you want later, okay?" I asked.

Mom threw the sleeves of her muumuu over her shoulders and reached out with two hands. Dad stood beside her and reached into the dimension. I tried to reach back. He shook his head. "Just stand there, Maggie-girl. I'm getting too much resistance."

I backed off, which fucking sucked, and let the parents handle the situation.

The portal opened like a surgeon's incision and through the tiny sliver, the world looked rich and full, dreamy like something you might view through a gauzy cheesecloth.

And then I felt this warm draw. It was really lovely. Killian got this blissed-out look on his face, too. I looked up and realized it was my mom, just shining her light out for us to follow. No wonder ghosts were always hanging around our house. If this is the way that things felt getting crossed over, I'd do it every day.

I stepped through as Dad held open the door. I reached behind me and grabbed Killian's hand and pulled him through, too.

We stepped out into the ballroom and Mom caught us both up in a hug, kissing our cheeks. She looked at me sternly. "Listen to me, young lady, I don't ever want to hear of you playing around in those realms again. Do you understand? My heart couldn't take having to cross you over again."

"I was standing just over there," I said, pointing at where the portal was. "We were fine."

Dad came over and smacked the back of my head.

"What have I told you about the dimensions other than The Other Side?"

I rubbed my scalp. "Hey, I didn't have any choice in the matter. Don't go yelling at me."

Mindy pushed her way through and wrapped her arms around my neck. "You're an idiot," she whispered.

Well, at least one person out of three was right.

I looked over at the door, and there was a little figure dressed in white who faded from solid into nothingness as the time bubble closed. I gave her a smile as she went. "Bye, Grandma," I said.

Mom looked at me. "What did you say?"

"Just... met someone over there I'd love to talk to you about," I smiled.

Suddenly, I got the weirdest prickling on the back of my neck. Like when you know someone is looking at you. I turned around and in the center of the ballroom was the bandstand, surrounded like an island in a seafood buffet. I looked up. There was Mortimer, dressed in a Hawaiian shirt beneath his tux tails, playing some absolutely terrible cover of Midnight at the Oasis. He gave me finger guns.

"Right back at you, guy," I smiled.

Killian whispered, "Should we report him to The Other Side authorities?"

I gave a shrug, my eyes never leaving America's newest star of the velvet night. "Eh. If someday they even figure out he's here, I figure we can let Lacy officially assign us and charge The Other Side a bucketload of money. Unofficially, I have never seen this man before in my life."

"Would we get to collect the directive in person?"

"Naturally!" I said as I wrapped my arm around

Killian's waist and gave him a good side squeeze. "I'm your partner, partner. You think I don't got your back?"

Killian smiled, "Never."

"Nice first case," I said. "I think I will keep you on."

"I think I will not quit."

"Good. Maybe we'll even get you a desk."

Killian nodded. "Perhaps something in an understated mahogany."

"Or maybe one that you've already got," said my dad, reaching over to shake Killian's hand.

"I think that, too, would be acceptable," he replied.

"Now, let's let this happy-go-lucky madman do what he has been looking forward to doing for decades," I said, nodding Mortimer's way. "And you and me go collect our moolah from Julio."

"I have been looking forward to that moment through the decades, too."

"I don't think he is going to be too happy we accomplished everything in time," I laughed. "Ain't life grand?"

Killian smiled back, "Absolutely divine."

"You two make the cutest couple!" piped up my mom. "Don't they, Mindy?"

Killian gave me a kiss on the top of my head. "Yes, we make excellent partners."

Fucking elves.

ACKNOWLEGEMENTS

As many of you long time readers know, this book was written as part of National Novel Writing Month with the majority of typing done at The Night of Writing Dangerously, an annual write-a-thon in San Francisco to benefit the Young Writers Program. The Young Writers Program provides free in-school creative writing classes and support. I began writing in the 4th grade, and so it holds a very special place in my heart.

It is with overwhelming gratitude that I thank my donors: Anne Auve, Caitlin Bergendahl, Cori Palladino, Joe Purcell, Richard Van Slyke, Tammy Turk, Debbie Valdivia, and Erika Wolbach. You helped a lot of kids and made this world a better place.

A special thanks to the Night of Writing Dangerously Angels who went above and beyond with their support: C.L. Jones, Corny Koehl, Christy & Tyler Wilhelm, and the Danley Family. BEYOND I SAY!

I did not come up with the title of this book. My Facebook followers did. In fact, the winning title came from the brain of Ray Stilwell. So thank you, Ray!

Putting together this book took a village. Special thanks to my Beta Reader of Awesome, Adam Jackman, and Proofreader of Pure Power, Raighne Kotrla (she didn't proofread this section, so any typeos here is pruely my own). Thanks to Mia and Ryan Winn for the ghost tour which inspired this whole mess. And a huge thank you to my family and friends for continuing to support me in all this madness.

But most of all, a special thank you to you. Yes, you. You, who pick up my books and say nice things and tell your friends. Don't tell anyone, but you have always been my favorite.

Thank you.

ABOUT THE AUTHOR

Kate Danley is a twenty year veteran of stage and screen with a B.S. in theatre from Towson University. She was one of four students to be named a Maryland Distinguished Scholar in the Arts.

Her debut novel, *The Woodcutter*, was honored with the Garcia Award for the Best Fiction Book of the Year, the 1st Place Fantasy Book in the Reader Views Literary Awards, and the winner of the Sci-Fi/Fantasy category in the Next Generation Indie Book Awards.

Her plays have been produced in New York, Los Angeles, and Maryland. Her screenplay *Fairy Blood* won 1st Place in the Breckenridge Festival of Film Screenwriting Competition in the Action/Adventure Category and her screenplay *American Privateer* was a 2nd Round Choice in the Carl Sautter Memorial Screenwriting Competition.

Her projects *The Playhouse, Dog Days, Sock Zombie, SuperPout*, and *Sports Scents* can be seen in festivals and on the internet. She trained in on-camera puppetry with Mr. Snuffleupagus and recently played the head of a 20-foot dinosaur on an NBC pilot. She has over 300+ film, theatre, and television credits to her name.

She lost on Hollywood Squares.

Sign up for her newsletter at
www.katedanley.com

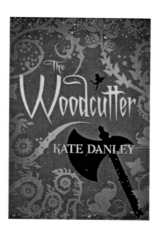

THE WOODCUTTER

Deep within the Wood, a young woman lies dead. No mark on her body. No trace of her murderer. Only her chipped glass slippers hint at her identity.

The Woodcutter, keeper of the peace between the Twelve Kingdoms of Man and the Realm of the Faerie, must find the maiden's killer before others share her fate.

But quickly he finds that one murdered maiden is not the only nefarious mystery afoot: one of Odin's hellhounds has escaped, a sinister mansion appears where it shouldn't, a pixie dust drug trade runs rampant, and more young girls go missing. Looming in the shadows is the malevolent, power-hungry queen, and she will stop at nothing to destroy the Twelve Kingdoms and annihilate the Royal Fae…unless the Woodcutter can outmaneuver her and save the gentle souls of the Wood.

Blending magic, heart-pounding suspense, and a dash of folklore, The Woodcutter is an extraordinary retelling of the realm of fairy tales.

Available on Amazon.com from 47North

MAGGIE MACKAY:
MAGICAL TRACKER

When monsters appear in Los Angeles, Maggie MacKay is on the job. No one is better at hauling the creepy crawlies back where they belong.

A snarky urban fantasy series from the mind of Kate Danley. The bad guys don't stand a ghost of a chance.

Maggie for Hire
Maggie Get Your Gun
Maggie on the Bounty
M&K Tracking (coming Fall 2013)

**Warning: This series contains
cussing, brawling, and unlady-like behavior.**

THE O'HARE HOUSE MYSTERIES

From the award winning author of The Woodcutter comes a spirited ghost story laced with Gothic tension, romance, and mystery.

Grieving widow Clara O'Hare accepts an invitation to a séance in the remote country home of Lord Horace Oroberg. Joining her around the table are Oroberg's cad of a son, Clifford; his mousy fiancée, Violet; her overbearing mother, Hilda Nero; Norman Scettico, a renowned scientist; the lovely Marguerite Matson; and the dashing young medium, Wesley Lowenherz.

Before long, the group's fascination with the spirit world calls up something sinister, and Clara and Wesley are pulled together to solve a murder most foul in a manor most spirited.

LIKE WHAT YOU READ?

- Tell your friends!

- Leave a nice review on Amazon, Goodreads, or B&N

- Follow Kate on Twitter @katedanley or Facebook

- Sign up for the Kate Danley newsletter at **www.katedanley.com** to hear about upcoming releases and sales

Thank you!

.

CPSIA information can be obtained at www.ICGtesting.com
Printed in the USA
LVOW10s0252211016

509697LV00012B/177/P